PRAISE FOR *AVA AND PIP*

"Through Ava's diary entries, Weston perfectly captures the complexities of sisterhood…a love letter to language."

—*New York Times* Book Review

"Ava Wren makes reading and writing so much fun, she deserves a T-O-P-S-P-O-T on your bookshelf. This charming diary will inspire shy kids, young writers, and even reluctant readers. Y-A-Y for A-V-A!"

—Dan Greenburg, author of the Zack Files series

"With her engaging voice, jaw-dropping word play, and tales of good people making not-so-good decisions, she casts the perfect spell. A big W-O-W for AVA and PIP!"

—Julie Sternberg, author of *Like Pickle Juice on a Cookie*

"[W]ill have readers cheering."

—*Booklist*

"Just enough conflict to keep the pages flying, with the comfortable certainty that it will all work out."

—*School Library Journal*

"You're gonna fall head over heels for the new book by our very own advice columnist Carol Weston."

—*Girls' Life*

"The charming story covers writing, sisterhood, and events that occasionally, says Ava, are 'making me feel like P-O-O-P.'"

—*Yale Magazine*

"Weston deals with family dynamics and creative challenges in realistic, emotionally honest ways."

—*Shelf Awareness*

"[A] witty, warm, wonderful story… As with all good books, I was both eager to find out, and reluctant to have it over, noting with sorrow the dwindling pages."

—Neil Steinberg, columnist at the *Chicago Sun-Times*

"Young readers will be enchanted with this endearing story about two very different sisters and their journey to find their voices."

—*Pittsburgh Post-Gazette*

"Such a wonderful book. It's so gratifying to see a child devour a book."

—Laura Ingraham

"Filled with funny word play, this clever story will grab anyone who has ever felt overlooked."

—*Discovery Girls*

"YAY!"

—Jon Agee, author of *The Incredible Painting of Felix Clousseau* and *Go Hang a Salami! I'm a Lasagna Hog!*

Also by Carol Weston

Ava and Pip

Ava and Taco Cat

AVA
XOX

Carol Weston

sourcebooks
jabberwocky

Copyright © 2016 by Carol Weston
Cover and internal design © 2016 by Sourcebooks, Inc.
Cover illustration © Victoria Jamieson

Sourcebooks and the colophon are registered trademarks of Sourcebooks, Inc.

Published by Sourcebooks Jabberwocky, an imprint of Sourcebooks, Inc.
P.O. Box 4410, Naperville, Illinois 60567-4410
(630) 961-3900
Fax: (630) 961-2168
www.sourcebooks.com

The Library of Congress Cataloging-in-Publication data is on file with the publisher.

Source of Production: Worzalla, Stevens Point, Wisconsin, USA
Date of Production: December 2015
Run Number: 5005338

Printed and bound in the United States of America.
WOZ 10 9 8 7 6 5 4 3 2 1

For Steve Geck

BEFORE DINNER

DEAR NEW DIARY,

I'm pretty upset about what happened today.

My new friend Zara asked if I'd heard about Chuck.

"No, what about him?" I said.

"He and Kelli are going out," she said.

"How do you know?" I asked because this did *not* seem possible, and, well, Zara has kind of a big mouth.

She said Chuck was on the bus minding his own business when Kelli hopped on and sat right next to him without asking. She was wearing one of her sparkly headbands—she has about a million—and sneaking bites of banana bread even though you're not supposed to eat on the bus. She offered him a piece. And he took it.

Later, in homeroom, Kelli passed Chuck a note that said, "Do you want to go out?" Zara said it had two circles, one marked YES and one marked NO. At first Chuck didn't answer, but Kelli made a sad puppy face, so he put an X in the YES circle and passed it back.

And now they are "going out"!!

I have to say, this really bugs me.

Number one: we're only in fifth grade.

Number two: Chuck and I have been friends since the apple-picking field trip in kindergarten, and Kelli just moved here last year, and I've never once noticed him notice her.

It just doesn't seem right that they've said about five sentences to each other—total—and all of a sudden they're "going out"! How long has she even liked him? Did she start *today*?

And how can they be going out when none of us is allowed to go anywhere anyway?

Lunch was spaghetti and meatballs, which I usually love, but my insides felt like cold, stuck-together spaghetti. It didn't help that Zara and my best friend Maybelle were talking about Valentine's Day, which is Saturday.

Our grade has three Emilys, but only one Ava, one Maybelle, and one Zara, and lately the six of us have been sitting together at lunch. Well, it's usually all-girl or all-boy, but today, Kelli plunked her tray down at Chuck's table! I was in shock! The Emilys just giggled, and Emily Jenkins said, "Kelli and Chuck make a good couple." And everyone agreed!

I swear, that made me want to throw up my meatballs. (Sorry if that's gross.)

The problem is that I'm not supposed to care as much as I guess I do. Last month, Zara asked if I liked Chuck, and I said no.

Why *do* I care anyway? Chuck is sweet and funny, but I think of him as a brother.

At least I *think* I think of him as a brother.

A sweet, funny brother.

Nothing more.

We're just friends.

H-U-H. That's a weird expression, isn't it? "*Just* friends." As though years of being friends is less important than *hours* of "going out."

AVA, ANNOYED

2/8
BEDTIME

DEAR DIARY,

One thing about Kelli: she's bubbly. Very bubbly. If you poured too much bubble bath in your bathtub and forgot to turn off the water, that's how much she bubbles. She's always laughing hysterically as if the whole world is a joke and she's the only one who gets it.

She also does splits and handstands and cartwheels at random times, which is impressive but show-offy. And she talks a lot about her lake house and vacations, which isn't polite considering the rest of us have one house, not two, and we have "staycations," not fancy trips. Another thing that bothers me is when Kelli's headband and fingernail polish match. (Today, they were emerald.)

She should take it down a notch.

Or move to a different school!

Anyway, when I got home today, Dad was taking out ingredients to make a yucky, squishy squash recipe for Meatless Monday (his new-ish tradition), so I told him a vegetable riddle:

Question: What room has no windows or doors?

4

Answer: A mushroom!

I asked if we could go to Bates Books so I could get a new diary—you!—and he said sure. (Dad likes that we're both writers.) I was glad because I *really* needed a place to dump all my feelings—as you can see because I've *already* filled five pages!

So far in my life, I have finished two diaries and given up on six. The unfinished ones are in a dead diary graveyard underneath my underwear.

I got my coat, and we drove over, and Dad and I walked inside the bookstore, and there were hearts everywhere! Red ones and pink ones. Big ones and little ones. Flat ones and 3-D ones and ones hanging from the ceiling. There were also Valentine's Day books, cards, pins, pens, mugs, magnets, stickers, and even giant heart doilies and heart-shaped boxes of chocolate. The owners of the bookstore are my friend Bea's parents, and she says they try to sell tons of holiday knickknacks so they can afford to keep selling regular books.

Confession: the happy hearts made me sort of sad.

I just can't believe Kelli asked Chuck out! And that this aggravates me so much.

Dad offered to buy me a box of Valentine cards, but I said no thanks. I told him that in second and third grade, our whole class used to exchange valentines, but now I'm too old.

"Too old?" Dad thought that was funnier than my mushroom riddle. "How about chocolate kisses? Are you too old for chocolate kisses?" He picked up a bag of chocolate kisses wrapped in silver and set it on the counter. Fortunately, moods are contagious, and Dad's good mood was helping me shake off my bad mood.

"I am the exact right age for chocolate kisses," I said, and on the way home, I unwrapped one for each of us.

AVA, AGGRAVATED

DEAR DIARY,

I just had the worst nightmare! I dreamed I was naked in school!! NAKED IN SCHOOL!!! I was in gym class and looked down and I wasn't wearing any clothes at all.

Not even any underwear!

Not even a...fig leaf! (That's what Adam and E-V-E wore.)

In my dream, I went racing full speed to the locker room and hid behind a shower curtain and held on tight. When I woke up, I was holding on to my *sheets* for dear life. And that's when I realized it was just a dream.

Phew!!

I think I had that dream because our gym teacher, Mrs. Kocivar, said that next year in sixth grade, girls can shower in school if they want to.

I will *never* want to!

AVA, WHO PREFERS PRIVACY

PS Mrs. Kocivar also showed us some modern dance steps and

said we should watch Kelli because she was doing it "perfectly." I made a little face and looked around to see if anyone else wanted to make a face back, but no one did. Am I the only person who doesn't think Kelli is perfectly perfect??

AFTER SCHOOL

DEAR DIARY,

Guess who I just ran into? Chuck!

Dad had to run some errands, so I went along. At the bank, I heard a crazy clinking clanking sound. I turned and there was Chuck pouring a bagful of pennies, nickels, dimes, and quarters into a giant sorting machine. When I went to say hi, it felt like my heart was beating as loudly as the machine. Which surprised me.

Since when do I feel nervous around Chuck?

Chuck said his mom said he could keep all the coins he found in their house and added, "But I bet she had *no* idea how many I would find!" He said he looked in pockets and drawers and under cushions and everywhere.

We waited together while the numbers kept going up, up, up. When they finally stopped, you know what the total was? $18.17!

"You're rich!" I teased. "What are you going to do with all that money?"

"I don't know."

"You could buy me bubblemint gum!"

He laughed and asked what my dad had cooked for "Barfy Monday." I told him squishy squash and made it sound extra gross, and then I was tempted to ask about his new girlfriend, but his mom came over and said they had to go. His mom always makes me nervous, probably because she is very tall and serious and has excellent posture.

Chuck is tall too, but he never used to make me nervous. He just made me laugh. While we were waiting for the noisy machine to count his money, for instance, he told me a joke that had a word from last Friday's spelling test: "Two *cannibals* were eating a clown, and one said to the other, 'Does this taste funny to you?'" (Hehe.)

I was glad he told it because it made things seem normal-ish between us even though I feel like they aren't.

Back home, our kitchen smelled scrumptious. Pip was baking gingerbread men (and gingerbread women and teens and kids and babies) with a seventh-grade girl named Tanya. Pip hardly ever has friends over, and I'd never met Tanya. Dad went upstairs, and I reached for a chocolate kiss, but the bowl was empty. I was about to say, "Pip, you ate *all* the chocolate kisses?!" when I realized Tanya must have helped.

If I had to describe Tanya, I guess I'd say that she is *pretty* but also *pretty* heavy. I've never really thought of this before, but Pip might be the smallest kid in seventh grade, and Tanya might be the... opposite?? It feels weird to write this down, and I don't mean that she's just a little chubby and who even cares? I mean that when she has checkups, I bet her doctor talks to her about weight and stuff.

Anyway, Tanya said that when she met our cat, she felt like she "already knew him" because of my story in the *Misty Oaks Monitor*, "The Cat Who Wouldn't Purr," which she'd "really liked."

"When did you adopt Taco Cat?"

"He was my birthday present on January 1 when I turned eleven."

She showed me two pencil sketches she'd made of him. They were both cute, and she'd even drawn in the white zigzag on his forehead and the white tip of his tail.

"You can have one," she said.

"Really?" I asked.

"Really."

I picked one and just now taped it on the rim of my mirror.

Hey, M-I-R-R-O-R-R-I-M is a palindrome! Which is funny because palindromes are sort of like words in mirrors since they're the same backward and forward.

I've never thought of M-I-R-R-O-R-R-I-M before, and trust me, I, A-V-A, sister of P-I-P, daughter of A-N-N-A and B-O-B, and owner of T-A-C-O-C-A-T, have thought of piles of palindromes.

Well, I helped Pip and Tanya take their gingerbread families out of the oven, and we let them cool. Then, minutes later, we started nibbling them, feet first, as though *we* were cannibals. Suddenly Pip said, "Whoa! We'd better save a few!" I think she realized it would have been bad if M-O-M or D-A-D walked into a yummy-smelling kitchen and found only ginger crumbs instead of ginger people.

After Tanya left, Pip told me that they were supposed to

have started their art project for Spanish but instead started baking and cutting out pastel hearts for a Valentine collage for Pip's boyfriend.

Sometimes I can hardly believe that Pip, who used to be so shy, has a real live valentine. And that he's *Ben Bates, Bea's Big Brother* (*al*literation *al*ert).

I can't imagine having a valentine.

(Or can I??)

AVA, AMBIVALENT (THAT'S WHEN YOU'RE NOT SURE)

2/10
BEFORE DINNER

DEAR DIARY,

Fifth grade is more complicated than fourth grade. Not just the math. *Everything*. It used to be that Maybelle was my best friend, and Chuck was my best guy friend, and that was that. Now Maybelle hangs out with Zara, and Chuck hangs out with Kelli, and I'm supposed to be okay with it all.

Even gym is complicated because some girls are "developing" and some aren't (like me). I think everyone is a little freaked out. The "mature" kids whose bodies are changing, and the other kids whose bodies are just sitting there. (Or standing or walking or running or whatever.)

Tomorrow we're starting a new class called FLASH. It stands for *F*amily *L*ife *A*nd *S*ocial *H*ealth. The funny thing is that our health teacher's name is Ms. *Sick*le. (Get it?)

It meets every Thursday.

My favorite class, of course, is English. Today Mrs. Lemons showed us something she'd printed from the Internet:

1 2 3 4 5 6 7 8 9 10 11 12 13 14 15
Re-post when you find the mitsake.

I kept looking and looking and was about to say, "I don't see any mistake" when I noticed it was a *spelling* "mitsake"—not a numbers one!

After class, Chuck and I started walking out the door together, the way we always used to, but there was Kelli waiting for him on the other side! I couldn't believe she came to meet him!! You might call that friendly, but I call it stalker-y! (Not that stalkers usually wear sparkly headbands.)

Chuck walked off with Kelli, and Zara looked at me like she could tell I was mad and sad.

Which I was.

Both.

I even mumbled, "I don't get what Chuck sees in her."

Without waiting a *single* *solitary* *second*, Zara said, "Well, she is pretty. And she's popular."

Popular? I've never really thought about popularity. Or maybe I thought popularity was something we didn't *have* to think about until puberty, which is something else I don't like to think about.

"And she's a good dancer," Zara continued. "And she's good at sports. And—"

Was Zara just getting warmed up? I put my hand in the air as if to say, "Stop!" Then I mentioned that in the girls' room, Kelli had applied lip gloss and announced that she likes "the natural look," and I'd wanted to say, "If you want to look natural, why wear makeup at all?"

Zara laughed, so I added, "I just hope Chuck doesn't get his feelings hurt."

Zara looked at me sideways as though she wasn't one hundred percent convinced this was my biggest concern.

AVA, CONCERNED

DEAR DIARY,

I just reread the Aesop's fable "Dog in the Manger." It goes like this:

A dog spends all afternoon napping on a pile of hay in a manger that belongs to an ox. At dusk, the ox comes home, and the dog wakes up. But he doesn't leave; he just stays there and barks and barks. At first, the hungry ox is patient, but finally he says, "Dog, since you aren't even eating my hay, why won't you let me have some?"

The moral: "Don't begrudge others what you yourself are not enjoying." Which means: don't be a selfish nincompoop for no good reason.

Am I being selfish about the Chuck-and-Kelli thing? It's not like Chuck and I were boyfriend-girlfriend, so why should I care who he goes out with?

Then again, I do care, whether I'm supposed to or not. Whenever I see Chuck, my insides lurch a little.

I went into Pip's room to talk, but she said, "Ava! Look!" and showed me the giant Valentine card she'd just finished for Ben.

She'd drawn HAPPY VALENTINE'S DAY in big balloon letters, and inside each, she'd glued the cut-out pastel hearts, and inside each of those, she'd written in tiny block letters "BE TRUE" and "YOU & ME" and "CUTIE PIE" and "CUPCAKE" and "SWEET TALK" and even "FIRST KISS."

She said she used the actual sayings from Sweethearts "conversation hearts"—but did *not* include "TRUE LOVE" because she didn't want to go overboard.

"Ben's going to love it!" I said and tried to feel happy for her instead of bad for me.

Then I wrote AVA and PIP and ANNA and BOB on a piece of paper and held it up to her mirror. "Look!"

"What?"

"My name is the coolest palindrome in our family because it's the only one that looks identical even in the mirror."

Pip studied the reflected words but shrugged as if it was no big deal, even though it kind of was. "Who cares?" she said.

"I do," I said and pointed out that WOW is a perfect palindrome too.

Pip shrugged and picked up the novel she was reading and said, "I have only three pages left." I knew that was code for "See you later, Alligator." So I took the hint and tried to find Taco because I felt a teeny bit lonely.

I thought of calling Maybelle, but it was too late, and besides, I haven't even told her that I am not happy about Chuck + Kelli. And maybe I shouldn't say anything because it seems like Maybelle + Kelli are becoming friends now too.

I guess everyone is falling under Kelli's sparkly spell—even the new science teacher. We did a unit on space and Kelli told our whole class all about a lunar eclipse she saw on one of her fancy vacations. And the teacher was just beaming.

AVA + TACO

PS Petting Taco helped…until he ran away.
PPS I bet it would be nice to like a boy who liked you back.
PPPS I wish I liked reading as much as Pip does. Whenever she wants to take her mind off things, she can enter a whole new world without even putting her shoes on. I'm a word nerd too, but I like writing more than reading, so the only world I ever hang out in is Misty Oaks.

IN THE LIBRARY

DEAR DIARY,

At breakfast, Mom asked us to sign a Valentine's card to go with a present for Nana Ethel. In my best handwriting, I wrote:

The Wren Family would like to say:

Happy Happy Valentine's Day!

Pip decorated it with flowers (mostly azaleas) and birds (mostly wrens).

We all four signed, and Pip added a paw print for Taco, and I added an XOX for kiss hug kiss. (Another perfect palindrome.)

Mom said, "Great job!"

But it was *not* a J-O-B. It was a J-O-Y.

Observation: one little letter can make a BIG difference!

I put the card in an envelope and asked if I should tape it on the present. Mom said, "No, tie it on," and handed me some ribbon.

"Is *that* a palindrome?" I asked and wrote it down: N-O-T-I-E-I-T-O-N. "Whoa! It is!" I announced and showed everyone.

"W-O-W," Mom said, so I showed her how WOW and MOM and AVA all look the exact same in the mirror, whereas

PIP and SIS and DAD do not. She smiled and said, "H-U-H, so they're symmetrical."

"Cool, right?" I said.

She nodded, and Dad said, "Do you ladies think Dr. Seuss was a word nerd?"

Pip said, "Definitely."

"Aha!" Dad continued in a teasing way. "But do you think he had Seuss issues?"

Mom and Pip looked puzzled, but I got it and said, "He definitely had Seuss issues! He had serious S-E-U-S-S-I-S-S-U-E-S!!"

Mom laughed and Dad high-fived me.

A-V-A, SYMMETRICAL

2/11
AFTER SCHOOL

DEAR DIARY,

Obviously, I believe in girl power and think girls should dream big and go after their goals, just like boys. But today Kelli wore a bright-pink Girl Power sweatshirt to school, and it bugs me that she acts all *entitled* and as if she *expects* to get whatever she wants.

Emily Sherman said that in third grade, Kelli's mom let her have a party at the Pampered Princess, an hour away. Everyone got manicures and pedicures and facials!

"What's a facial?" I asked.

"It's when someone rubs cream on your cheeks and puts cucumber slices on your eyelids to help you relax."

"Oh." I tried to remember third grade. Did I need creams and cucumbers to relax? I'm pretty sure I could relax by jumping rope or watching videos or hanging out with Pip or Maybelle or…Chuck.

Speaking of, at lunch, Kelli sat at a table near ours, and when Chuck walked by, she said, "Chuck! I saved you a seat!" So he sat down with her.

Confession: it took away my appetite.

Zara says Kelli's been saving him a seat on the bus home from school every day too.

Does Chuck even *want* to sit next to Kelli all the time?

Should I ask him?

And why do I care as much as I obviously do? *Do* I like-like my friend Chuck??

In FLASH, Ms. Sickle said feelings can be messy.

I think she's right. It would be easier if when you liked a person, that person liked you back the exact same amount in the exact same way, and that was that.

Ms. Sickle broke us into groups and had us flip through women's magazines. She said we should look for pages that show "mixed and contradictory messages." At first we didn't know what she meant. But then it was "eye-opening" because the magazines had ads for candy bars and recipes of gooey desserts *right next* to articles on how to "shed pounds fast." Ms. Sickle said it's hard to "live mindfully" in a world full of temptations, but it's important to try.

AVA, OPEN-EYED?

2/11
TWENTY MINUTES LATER

DEAR DIARY,

There's something I didn't tell you, and now I'm almost embarrassed to, even though you're my private diary. But writing helps, so here goes:

At the end of the day, I had to pee, so I went to the girls' room and dashed in and out and didn't notice that I'd stepped on a piece of toilet paper. I ran to where Pip usually meets me after school, and two older kids were pointing at my feet and smirking. One was Loudmouth Lacey, that girl who wears thick eyeliner and used to pick on Pip. The other was an eighth grader named Rorie who everyone says is mean. (She looks like she could beat people up without even trying.)

Chuck must have noticed, because he came over and mumbled, "TP alert."

"Huh?" I said. (I did not spell it out.)

He pointed at my left boot, and I glanced down and saw the tissue trail and thought, *OMG! TP?* I mumbled thanks and stepped on the tissue with my right boot. The TP came off, but so did what was left of my *dignity*.

When I looked up, Chuck was gone—probably already on the bus next to Kelli, who would never be caught dead dragging TP around. (Not that *I* was *literally* "caught dead." I mean, I'm still breathing.)

Anyway, Pip showed up with Tanya, and my face must have been toilet-paper white, because Pip said, "What's the matter?"

All I could say was, "Nothing."

Ava, Nothing

PS One of tomorrow's spelling test words is *humiliated*.

2/11
BEDTIME

DEAR DIARY,

After school, Tanya and Pip worked on their homework poster. So I made a poster too. I made mine for Bates Books, and in my best handwriting, I wrote: "Books are gifts you can open again and again." I even added, "Buy Local," because Bea said it drives her parents crazy when people browse for books at their store and then order them online. Mrs. Bates says she wishes they'd worry about "saving their community," not just "saving every dollar." She also says bookstores give towns "character," which is funny since bookstores are full of books that are full of characters.

Anyway, we made popcorn, but Tanya melted half a stick of butter and poured it all over the top, and it ended up *too* buttery.

After Tanya left, I told Pip about the toilet paper, and she said, "That's happened to everybody," which made me feel better. Then Pip told me what *she* is worrying about. It's way bigger than tagalong TP.

Last week, Pip's Spanish class got divided up into pairs, and one kid from each pair had to reach into a hat and pick out a name of an artist from a Spanish-speaking country. "One kid got Picasso," Pip said. "Another got Goya. Another got Frida Kahlo. Another got El Greco. Another got Velázquez. And Tanya picked for us and got Botero." (I had to look up those spellings.)

Pip said each pair of kids is supposed to give a short talk and make a poster of one of their artist's paintings.

"So? What's the *problema*?" (That's "problem" in Spanish.)

"We have to do our presentations during an assembly in front of the whole middle school!"

"But in English, right?"

"Duh."

"And for kids, not parents, right?"

"Right."

"You can do it, Pip!" I said, because Pip really has come out of the shell she used to be all scrunched up inside.

Then again, it was still hard to picture Pip talking in front of such a big group.

"It's not just me. It's Tanya." Pip lowered her voice as if she didn't even want to say what she was about to say. "We were talking about height and weight, and she…she…told me she wears size XXXL."

I waited. Pip is not the kind of person who judges people on their appearance. She doesn't even judge books by their covers.

Pip pushed her art book toward me. "Look."

I looked, and it was open to the Botero paintings. Well, it turns out that Botero has a very particular style. Someone could probably walk right into a museum and say, "I bet Botero painted that!" He paints all his subjects larger than life. There was a big round king, and a big round princess, and a big round dancer, and a big round bullfighter. Suddenly I understood the *problema*. Botero paints big people, and Tanya is…not small.

"Oh," I said.

"I just hope no one says anything," Pip said. "Tanya's pretty insecure. One of her cousins makes fun of her."

"That's terrible," I said.

Pip showed me the poster that they'd finished drawing and coloring. They'd done a really good job copying the *Mona Lisa*. But it was not the *Mona Lisa* that Leonardo da Vinci painted hundreds of years ago. It was a *Mona Lisa* that Botero painted much more recently.

Oh, I'll just come out and say it. Botero's *Mona Lisa* is… *chubby*. Instead of an oval, her face is a circle. Her cheeks and chin and neck are big, and her eyes and nose and mouth are small.

We were both quiet, and I got an idea. "Pip, I could make Tanya a valentine, an anonymous one."

"Like from a secret admirer?"

"Not lovey-dovey, just nice. And unsigned. Maybe it would boost her confidence?"

"I don't think it's that easy. But sure, if you want." Pip went back to her homework, and I made a heart-shaped valentine for Tanya that I'm going to sneak into her locker tomorrow. It says:

Happy Valentine's Day to a very sweet person!

I decorated it with red balloons and red lollipops—though I'm not sure you can tell which are which.

AVA, MORE ALTRUISTIC THAN ARTISTIC (*ALTRUISTIC* MEANS WANTING TO HELP)

Dear Diary,

I dreamed I made a valentine for Chuck but was too embarrassed to give it to him.

Question one: Do boys ever dream about girls?

Question two: Do I wish Chuck were *my* valentine?

Since you are my diary and no one else will ever read this, I guess I will admit that I think I do.

Okay, yes, I do.

I do.

I *do* like Chuck.

Wait, all those "I do's" make it sound like we're getting married!!

All I mean is that I realize that when I think about Chuck, I *keep thinking* about him. He doesn't just cross my mind; he finds a chair and sits right down!

And usually that's okay, because thinking about him makes me smile. Lately, though, it makes me frown.

Is he telling Kelli jokes and making her laugh? Does he think about her as much as I think about him?

AVA :-(

FIFTH PERIOD, IN THE LIBRARY

DEAR DIARY,

After homeroom, I went to the bathroom and was about to come out of the stall when I recognized Kelli's and Zara's voices. Kelli said, "Isn't Chuck soooo cute? Do you think he's the tallest boy in fifth grade?"

Zara said, "Maybe. Or maybe tied with Jamal?"

"I can't wait for my party!" Kelli said. "Should I invite the whole grade?"

Zara said, "If your parents will let you, why not?"

"Oh, there are a few kids I could do without!" She laughed, and I wondered who she meant. Did she mean *me*? I don't like her, but does she not like *me*? And if so, is it because Chuck and I are…friends?

Well, I couldn't just poke my head out, so I had to stay hidden until the coast was clear. And it was awkward sitting there, trapped. Plus, Mrs. Hamshire gets mad if you're even two seconds "tardy."

Finally Zara and Kelli must have had to pee, because they went into the stalls on either side of me. The second they closed the doors, I made a run for it—and a beeline to math class.

At lunch, Kelli announced that she was having a Valentine's party, and now that's all anybody can talk about. It's our grade's *first* boy-girl party—if you don't count all the ones we had when we were little.

I wish the party weren't at Kelli's.

I also wish I had the guts to give Chuck a card—or collage.

But he's *not* my valentine, so that would be *inappropriate*!

AVA, APPROPRIATE

DEAR DIARY,

Taco Cat and I were on the sofa, and Pip was on the floor working on her new book, *Z Is for Zinnia*. She's made three pages: A is for azalea, B is for buttercup, and C is for chrysanthemum. (Note: *chrysanthemum* is a hard spelling word, which is one reason most people just say "mum.")

Anyway, P-I-P was filling in the petals of her M-U-M and making them R-E-D-D-E-R and R-E-D-D-E-R (palindrome alert!), and I asked if Tanya had said anything about getting a valentine.

Pip said, "No, but she did ask me a personal question."

"What?"

"She said, 'Didn't you used to be shy? Like *really* shy?'" Pip looked at me. "I didn't answer right away, but she kept asking how I got less shy, so I ended up telling her the whole story about how you and Bea made those five Pip Pointers to help me get braver."

"You told her about the five Pip Pointers??"

"Yes. And you know what she said? She said she wished she

had ten Tanya Tips to help her lose weight because she knows she's not 'the prettiest flower in the garden.'"

"She *said* that?" I made a sad little "Oh" sound. It just came out. "What did you say?"

"I didn't know *what* to say! I objected and everything. But Tanya said that all her relatives—except her grandmother—used to say, 'Look how big you are!' like it was a compliment, and then one day she noticed that, without any warning, that sentence went from being a good thing to a bad thing."

"That's awful!"

"I know. So I said I'd ask you."

"*Me?*"

"You and Bea."

I scrunched my face and pointed out that Bea and I don't know anything about losing weight. "Bea only knew about shyness because her brother Ben used to be shy."

"He's not anymore," Pip said and smiled to herself. Then she added, "Oh, c'mon, Ava. You told me Bea wants to be an advice columnist."

"Yeah, but someone who *wants* to be a pilot can't fly an airplane," I protested. "And someone who *wants* to be a doctor can't perform an operation. And someone who *wants* to be a boxer can't—"

"Can't you and Bea just give it a try?" Pip asked, interrupting. "I bet it took a lot of guts for Tanya to ask."

"Let me think about it," I said.

AVA, CORNERED

2/12
BEDTIME

DEAR DIARY,

At dinner, I told Mom and Dad that I got another 100 on our Friday spelling test. Dad said, "Way to go!" and Mom said, "Good for you!" (They used to forget to say things like that.)

What I didn't say out loud is that when we graded the tests, Chuck and I traded papers—and this was the highlight of my whole day.

One of the words was *handkerchief,* and Chuck wrote *Kleenex.* I thought that was really creative and he should get at least partial credit. But Mrs. Lemons said to mark it wrong. He also got *earnest* and *sincere* wrong. Another word was *palindrome,* which of course I know backward and forward. Another was *afterthought,* which I sometimes used to feel like at home back when Mom and Dad were always worrying about Pip. One last word was *valentine.*

When Chuck gave me back my test, he drew a big star around the 100. When I gave back his, I did not circle the 70, but I did whisper, "You got *palindrome* and *valentine* right."

He whispered, "Did you hear about Kelli's party this weekend?"

I nodded.

He said, "You going?"

I nodded again.

He said, "Me too."

Maybe I should have left well enough alone, but I didn't. I whispered, "Are you and Kelli really going out?" I could *not* believe I said that!

He looked like he couldn't either. His eyes went wide, and he turned a little pink. "Sort of."

Mrs. Lemons said, "No talking." She looked right at us and added, "Or whispering."

I passed Chuck a note: "Sort of?"

He turned the note over, scribbled on it, and pushed it back to me. It said, "1. I'm not aloud to go out." (He wrote "aloud," but I knew he meant *allowed*.)

Then he ripped a second strip of paper from his notebook and wrote "2." He was about to scribble something else, but the bell rang, and You-Know-Who was already peeking in the little window in the door. (If you don't know, I'll give you a hint: she was wearing a sparkly sunshine-yellow headband.)

AVA, NOTE PASSER

PS What was Chuck going to write in his second note??

2/13
SATURDAY MORNING

DEAR DIARY,

There's no school on Monday because of Abraham Lincoln's and George Washington's birthdays. I cannot tell a lie: I love three-day weekends!

Y-A-Y presidents!

I also like that it's not getting dark quite so early. But it's still icy cold out. Today I went outside to bring in the newspaper, and I could see my breath.

Valentine's Day is tomorrow, and the whole grade is going to Kelli's. She said all the girls should wear red or pink. I don't own anything pink, but Pip has a top I can borrow that is not too girlie-girlie.

This morning Pip asked me if I'd talked to Bea yet, and I had to admit that I hadn't. She said I should and handed me her cell phone, with the number already pressed in.

Bea answered, and I said hi, and she said, "What's up?"

"The ceiling," I replied, but then felt immature since Bea is two years older than me. So I just went ahead and told her that Pip talked to Tanya about the Pip Pointers and now Tanya wants us to come up with Tanya Tips—but about weight loss. I thought Bea might say, "Tanya's weight is not my problem" or "What do I know?" But Bea said Tanya was one of the first kids who was nice to her when she moved to Misty Oaks and added, "I didn't know her weight bothered her."

"Want to come over?" I asked.

"One sec," Bea said, and I heard a muffled conversation. Then she said, "Or you and Pip can come to the bookshop. Ben and I are about to go there."

I ran that idea by Pip, and she liked it and jumped in the shower. Now she's drying her hair with a blow-dryer and just asked loudly, "Should I give Ben the valentine I made?"

"Definitely," I shouted back, Little Miss Love Expert.

"Think he'll have one for me?" she shouted.

"I don't know if boys are as into Valentine's Day as girls," I shouted back. "But he could always grab one from the card rack."

Pip shouted, "That's real romantic."

I rolled up my poster and put it in my backpack and mumbled, "At least you're giving your valentine to a boy. I'm giving mine to a store."

AVA, WHOSE CRUSH IS SOMEONE ELSE'S VALENTINE

PS I didn't mean to write "CRUSH," but it was like my hand had a mind of its own. (Wait. Can *hands* have *minds?*)

DEAR DIARY,

We entered the bookstore, and Mrs. Bates put my poster by the register, which made me feel good.

Bea and Ben came over, and we went to the back and put our coats and hats and scarves and gloves in a big clothes puddle in the corner. Then Pip gave Ben her handmade valentine, and he handed her a great big red envelope! It *was* romantic! Especially since Bates Books is practically polka-dotted with hearts.

Ben and Pip stayed in the kids' section, and Bea and I walked to a grown-up section. Meow Meow, their friendly Creamsicle-colored cat, followed us, his tail high in the air.

I have to say: I'd never noticed how many books are in Bates Books. I guess I'd always hung out in the kids' area, but there are shelves and shelves of books for grown-ups.

Mrs. Lemons once told us about genres—like mysteries and sci-fi and fantasy and graphic novels and historical fiction and realistic fiction (my favorite). But most books are nonfiction. And a lot of them have to do with food.

I'm not kidding. Bates Books sells hundreds of cookbooks.

Some explain how to cook French or Italian or Greek or Mexican or Indian or Chinese meals. Some explain how to cook soup or fish or meat or vegetables or dessert. Some are for beginners, some are for experts, some are for people with allergies. And they're all bursting with recipes and photos! They're like picture books for grown-ups.

Right next to the cookbooks are diet books. Tons of them! There are almost as many books about *not* eating as there are about eating! It made me think of when Ms. Sickles had us look for "mixed and contradictory messages." Bea said they have books about eating disorders too, like when people eat so much, they make themselves sick, or starve themselves and have to go to the hospital.

"I think Tanya wants just general suggestions," I said.

We sat on the floor and started looking at self-help books on "wellness," and I started writing down tips. Bea said her mom and dad don't like it when kids treat the bookstore as if it's a "lending library," but they don't mind if *she* does.

I told her that if we come up with a good list for Tanya, I might make a poster for FLASH class. I also told her that Ms. Sickle just put up a poster with a giant B+ and, underneath, the words: "*Be positive.*"

Bea smiled, and Meow Meow rubbed up against my knee and hopped onto my lap and started purring and purring like there was no place he'd rather be. (Taco never does that.) "He's such a good cat," I said.

"I know," Bea said.

We kept leafing through books and talking, and I took notes like: "If you drink sugary soda, try to switch to water." And "If you tend to eat fast, try to put down your fork between some bites." And "Leave the ice cream in the grocery store because it's much easier to resist temptation *once* in a store than all day long at home." I also wrote "Use smaller plates," and "Take the stairs not the elevator," and "Go places by bike, not car," which is exactly what Pip and I had just done even though it had meant bundling up with hats, scarves, and gloves.

Besides all the practical tips, Bea said her aunt—the psychotherapist—would say to think "big picture."

"Big picture?"

"Like, picture yourself in better shape so you're 'visualizing success,' rather than just 'feeling deprived.'"

I nodded, and Bea kept dictating tips like, "Avoid high-fructose corn syrup." And "Don't expect to drop pounds over-night." And "Give yourself lots of credit for trying to take better care of yourself."

It was fun to be working with Bea again. Interesting too, because I'd never thought about *c*arbs, *c*alories, or *c*orn syrup.

It reminded me of when we made the Pip Pointers, back when Pip could hardly say hi to people.

I guess we all have different strengths and weaknesses.

One of my strengths is spelling. I can spell *carbohydrate* even though I'm not exactly sure what it means.

One of my weaknesses is math. I wish I could remember numbers the way I can remember letters. But everyone's brain is different. Chuck once joked: "There are *three* kinds of people in this world—those who can count and those who can't."

One of Pip's strengths is drawing and another is concentration. When she reads, she's in another world. Sirens could be blaring all around, and she wouldn't hear them. Another strength is her sense of direction. The only place *she* gets lost is inside books!

Well, this might be another one of my weaknesses (or maybe it's normal?), but once something starts to bother me, it's hard for me to stop thinking about it every single second. So another nice thing about being with Bea was that it got my mind off Kelli and her sparkly headbands and perfect backflips and princess parties and how she stole Chuck away from me (even though he was never mine in the first place and she probably didn't know I liked him, since *I* barely knew).

After a while, Meow Meow jumped off my lap and climbed onto the pile of clothes to take a catnap while Bea and I put all the books back. I thought about asking Bea what to do if you have a crush on a boy who is "taken" *and* who used to be your best guy friend. But I didn't.

When you hang out with older kids, it's better not to remind them of how immature you are.

On the bike ride home, Pip led the way but seemed upset, which was weird because she'd been so happy an hour earlier.

"What's wrong?" I shouted.

She didn't say, "Nothing," which meant, "Something." When we got home, she went straight to her room and closed the door.

I went into my room and spent a little time with my stuffed

animals. Sometimes I worry that I'm neglecting them. But now that I'm eleven, I guess it makes sense that I don't play with Winnie the Pooh all day.

H-U-H. I just thought of something. If Winnie owned a hula hoop, it would be Pooh's hoop or P-O-O-H-S-H-O-O-P.

I wonder what's bugging P-I-P anyway.

A-V-A, L-I-L S-I-S

DEAR DIARY,

I got a haircut today. A bob (B-O-B)!

Maybelle is about to come over for a sleepover. Y-A-Y for BFFs!

Dad showed me some words that come out funny if you re-arrange their letters, so I'm taping in my favorites:

WORDS	SAME WORDS WITH REARRANGED LETTERS
THE EYES	THEY SEE
ASTRONOMER	MOON STARER
SNOOZE ALARMS	ALAS NO MORE Z'S
A DECIMAL POINT	I'M A DOT IN PLACE
THE MORSE CODE	HERE COME DOTS
DORMITORY	DIRTY ROOM
LISTEN	SILENT

I started looking for words inside AVA ELLE WREN and found lots, like EVER and NEVER and REVEAL and ALL NEW.

AVA ELLE WREN, ALL NEW

PS You know what TACO is scrambled? COAT. And you know what TACO CAT scrambled is? CAT COAT or...fur!

DEAR DIARY,

Maybelle conked out (maybe because she does a lot of sports all week), but I couldn't fall asleep, so I'm writing in you with the light-up pen that Bea gave me last year.

It's funny. A lot of people like to read at night, but I like to write at night.

Anyway, dinner was chicken potpie, and Pip was as quiet as in the olden days. The rest of us started talking about pen names or *pseudonyms*. Like Mark Twain's real name was Samuel Clemens. And Lewis Carroll's real name was Charles Dodgson. And Lemony Snicket's is Daniel Handler.

Mom also talked about a cat with kidney failure that Dr. Gross had to "put down." She said their office always sends out a condolence note after a pet dies, but today's made her sad because the lady was eighty-six and the cat's name was Valentine.

Dad changed the subject away from dead pets and asked Maybelle about soccer and Mathletes. Maybelle answered, then said she'd brought us each a box of "conversation hearts"—and me a bag of gummy bears.

Next thing you know, Mom and Dad both found a heart that said "MARRY ME," and gave them to each other, which was pretty...sweet.

Maybelle said the Sweethearts company makes two *billion* hearts a year.

Mom and Dad seemed impressed, but Pip just shrugged.

After dinner, Pip, Maybelle, and I went upstairs, so I said, "Pip, you should show Maybelle the valentine Ben gave you!"

Pip said, "That's the last thing I want to do."

"Oh, come on!"

"No way!"

"Yes way! Why not?"

"Because!"

"Because what?"

Maybelle began to squirm. She's an only child and doesn't get that sister fights are not that big a deal. Personally, I think Pip *wanted* to show us but also wanted me to beg. I wasn't even surprised when, two minutes later, she said, "Oh fine. Come in, but close the door behind you."

We went into her room, and Taco scurried in too. He sniffed Maybelle's socks but did not climb onto her lap and start purring up a storm, like Meow Meow.

Pip took out the valentine. The envelope was even bigger than I remembered! It was giant, and the card inside was shaped like a bouquet of roses!

"Whoa," Maybelle said.

"So what's the matter?" I asked. I can tell when my sister is upset. I've known her since the day I was born. (She was two years, two months, and two weeks old when she met me—not that either of us remembers.)

"Read what he wrote," she said. We did. And it did not take long at all because what Ben wrote was just three words (four if you count his name).

After I read the words, I said, "Oh."

Maybelle read the words aloud: "I love you." She looked from me to Pip and didn't seem to get what the problem was. But I did. Obviously, D-A-D, M-O-M, P-I-P, and I take words (not just palindromes) very seriously, and LOVE is a very serious word!

For instance, I think about Chuck a lot (too much?), but I'd never, ever write "I love you" on a valentine!

I guess it can be tricky to put feelings into words. Maybe that's why so many Valentine cards mostly have pictures of kittens (and puppies and bunnies and ducklings) that make you melt and go "Awww."

"So what *did* you say?" I asked.

"I thanked him for the card," Pip said.

"You didn't say it back?" Maybelle asked.

Pip shook her head sadly.

"Did he notice that you didn't?" I asked.

"I think so."

"*Do* you love him?" I asked really quietly.

Pip squinted. "Isn't love for when we're older?"

"Ben *is* in eighth grade," Maybelle pointed out.

"Well, I didn't feel right saying it. So I didn't."

Maybelle and I stayed silent. Taco put his head under his paw.

"But I guess I should say…something," Pip added.

"Want us to talk to him for you?" I asked. "I could tell Bea to tell Ben—"

"NO!" Pip shouted before even I realized that this was a moronic idea.

Taco darted out the door, and I mumbled, "Just trying to help."

"I know," Pip said. "But, Ava, you have to be careful! It's not enough to have good intentions." Obviously she was referring to the boneheaded "Sting of the Queen Bee" story I wrote last fall when I felt bad for Pip after her birthday party got canceled. (Bea had thrown a huge boy-girl party on the same day that Pip was having her slumber party—but Bea hadn't done it on purpose.) "And don't tell Mom and Dad!"

"I won't."

"I don't want them worrying that Ben and I are getting too serious. Because we aren't!"

"Okay!" I said a little huffily.

"Think I should text him?" Pip asked.

"*Maybe,*" *Maybe*lle said.

Pip sighed as if she couldn't believe she was asking fifth graders for advice on her love life—or *not-love* life.

She took a breath, picked up her cell phone, and started to type. Then she showed us what she wrote: "Dear Ben, I ♥ you but I don't feel ready to use the L word. I hope that's okay. Please don't take it personally because I like you as much as I've ever liked any boy. Happy Valentine's Day!"

"That's good," I said and tried to imagine texting Chuck something like that someday. (Not that I even have a cell phone!)

"Should I press Send?" she asked.

We nodded and…she did.

Then we all sat there and stared at her phone.

Nothing happened.

"He might be playing video games," Maybelle said after a minute.

"Or at a movie," I said.

"Or eating dinner with his parents," Maybelle said.

"Or doing homework," I added.

Pip looked worried and reread the text she'd sent. To distract her, I said, "You should show Maybelle *Z Is for Zinnia*!"

Pip nodded and got out her book project. Since I'd last seen it, she had drawn F is for foxglove, G is for geranium, H is for hollyhock, and I is for iris.

"You're such a good artist!" Maybelle gushed, so Pip got out the Botero poster and showed it to her too.

Maybelle took one look and laughed out loud. "Hahaha! That's hysterical! A tubby *Mona Lisa*!"

Pip snatched back the poster, rolled it up, and said, "It's not supposed to be 'hysterical.'"

Maybelle looked at me, confused, and apologized to Pip.

I felt bad for both of them.

Soon Maybelle and I went downstairs and made P-O-P P-O-P P-O-P popcorn. I told her that Pip is nervous because in three days, she and Tanya have to talk in front of the whole middle school.

"Who's Tanya?" Maybelle asked, and I described her. "Oh, I know! Chubby, but a pretty face, right?"

I nodded and wondered if Tanya knew that this was probably how most people described her. *Nice* people, anyway. Who knows what not-nice people said? (Poor Tanya!)

I watched as Maybelle attempted to pour the popcorn equally into two bowls. She was taking a long time, so I teased, "You could count the kernels."

She threw a piece of popcorn at me, and I tossed it up in the air and tried to catch it in my mouth, but I missed.

"Do you think people ever love each other the exact same amount?" I asked as I picked up the piece of popcorn.

"I don't think love is something you can quantify," she answered.

We both laughed because that was such a Maybelle thing to say. (Math is one of her strengths!)

But *is* love lopsided? Is it like an out-of-balance seesaw? Does one person always like the other one more?

And will tomorrow's Valentine's Day party be fun?

AVA, ASKING

2/13
A LITTLE LATER

DEAR DIARY,

Maybelle is still asleep, and I'm still awake, so I got Bea's light-up pen back out because I wanted to write down a joke Dad told me:

Question: Why should you never use a dull pencil?

Answer: Because it's pointless.

H-O-H-O-H-O-H

AVA, AWAKE

PS I can't believe I'm still awake. Am I nervous about the party? Is my crush *pointless*?

2/14
VALENTINE'S DAY MORNING

DEAR DIARY,

Maybelle's mom picked her up early, so I hung out in the kitchen with Dad, and we made heart-shaped pancakes while Mom and Pip slept in. I framed each stack with sliced strawberries and set the table with red cloth napkins. Dad sizzled eight strips of bacon to perfection, and I called, "Breakfast!"

Mom came downstairs and said, "Mmm, smells good." She was right. The kitchen smelled of bacon and maple syrup.

Pip came down next and brought her cell phone with her. I guess she's still hoping Ben will text back. But what if his feelings got hurt? He's probably never written "I love you" to anyone. He was probably hoping she'd just say it back and that would be that. (Observation: when Kelli asked Chuck to go out, he didn't leave her hanging; he said yes back, and that *was* that. Stupid Kelli!)

When we were all sitting down, I looked at Mom and Dad and asked, "Do you guys love each other the same amount?"

Mom looked startled, and Pip glared at me, but Dad put down his coffee and said, "Great question." Then he said, "Love means different things to different people. But I think we do. Mind you, Mom likes to hold her cards close to the chest."

Pip looked confused and said, "H-U-H?" (Funny how my family really does spell out H-U-H when we're talking to each other. It's like a weird inside joke.)

"It's an expression," Dad said. "If you're playing poker and don't want people to know if you have a royal flush—or a pair of deuces—you hold your cards close to your chest."

"Deuces?" I asked.

"Twos," Dad replied.

"What Dad means," Mom said, "is that I don't go on and on as much as some people."

I realized that this was true. Like Dad might say, "This book is pure genius!" but Mom never would. If Mom and Dad were teachers, Dad would be a much easier grader.

"Which of you said 'I love you' first?" I asked. Pip kicked me under the table. But I wasn't talking about Ben and Pip. I was talking about Mom and Dad.

Dad said, "That's pretty personal, sweetie, but I'll tell you. In college, when I was a senior and Mom was a sophomore, I told her I loved her on our third date. I meant it too. She didn't say it back for *months*. I wasn't worried though. I knew she found me irresistible!"

He smiled at Mom, and she giggled as though they were still in college. She even tossed her napkin at Dad, which was funny. They don't usually throw stuff at each other.

AVA, WHO ASKED

PS Do Chuck and Kelli like each other the same amount?

PPS Do *I* like Chuck and Taco both more than they like me?

PPPS Will Kelli's Valentine's Day party be *aw*esome or *aw*ful?

DEAR DIARY,

Pip was working on her Spanish homework and suddenly said, "Ava, I just learned a Spanish palindrome."

"What?" I asked.

"*O-S-O.*"

"What does it mean?"

She told me.

"*Bare?*" I asked. "Like *bare* naked?"

"No. B-E-A-R. Like *bear* hug."

"Oh," I said.

"Oh-so," she said, because that's how you pronounce *oso*.

"Want to hear a bear joke?" I asked.

"Sure," she said but rolled her eyes to show that fifth-grade humor is beneath her.

"What do you call a bear with no teeth?" I asked.

"What?"

"A *gummy bear!*" I said. Before she could groan, I ran into my room and grabbed her a few gummy bears.

"Aw, thanks," she said.

"For Valentine's Day," I said.

O-X-O (which is hug kiss hug)

Ava the Sweet

PS I wonder what age people are supposed to be before they can give each other bear hugs.

2/14
4 P.M.

Dear Diary,

Pip's cell phone rang, and she jumped and read it and smiled big-time. It was a text from Ben, and soon they were texting back and forth. Later Pip showed me what they wrote—which was lucky because otherwise I might have been tempted to sneak a peek while she was in the shower!

He texted: "It's OK. We can just ♥ each other."

She texted a pink heart emoticon.

He texted: "PS My battery was dead and I couldn't find the charger. Sorry!"

She texted another pink heart.

He texted: "What are you doing later?"

She texted "idk" which means "I don't know." And then he called! And they made a plan to go skating! Today! On Valentine's Day!

I wonder if they will hold hands. Like whoever skates better can make sure the other one doesn't fall? Or maybe they'll skate and skate and not touch at all? (A rhyme!)

I can alllllllmost picture myself skating with Chuck. But I can't picture us holding hands.

Kelli's party starts in an hour. I don't know if I'm ready for a real boy-girl party, especially at Kelli's. And especially since, as I confessed, I ♥ Chuck a little even though I'm not supposed to.

AVA, INAPPROPRIATE

2/14
RIGHT BEFORE THE PARTY

DEAR DIARY,

Why *do* I ❤ Chuck anyway? Sometimes he is gross. For example, here's a joke he told me that I can't get out of my head:

Question: What do people who eat lots and lots of alphabet soup have?

Answer: Vowel movements.

At first I didn't get it. Then I said, "Ewww!"

I just told that joke to Pip and asked if she thought it was funny or disgusting. She said, "Both," and explained that a lot of middle school boys have sick senses of humor. She said that last week, a boy in her science class said, "It's better to be 'pissed off' than 'pissed on.'"

"Ugh!" I said, shocked by the joke and the fact that Pip knows so much about middle school boys.

She also said, "What's the difference between roast beef and pea soup?"

"What?" I asked.

"Anyone can roast beef," she said.

I said "Ewww!" again and rolled my eyes.

Then I asked if she was still nervous about her presentation

58

in the assembly next week. She said yes but added that she was *not* going to think about it on Valentine's Day. I asked if I could borrow her pink top and she said sure.

AVA IN PINK

PS It's not that I like all of Chuck's jokes. What I like is that he picks them out just for me. Or he used to anyway.

2/14
VALENTINE'S DAY NIGHT

DEAR DIARY,

When I walked into Kelli's big modern house, the whole place smelled like pizza. A lady in a uniform took my coat and put it in Kelli's room, and a younger blond lady said, "Come in! Come in!" I figured she was Kelli's mother.

All the girls in my grade were wearing pink or red except Emily Jenkins, who forgot. I'm glad I didn't forget. I would not have wanted to be wearing yellow if everyone else was wearing pink and red.

I looked around and did not see Chuck anywhere.

Kelli was wearing a white top with red hearts and golden heart earrings. (She's one of the only girls in our class with pierced ears.) Her headband was red with shiny sequins. Even her dog had little red bows. She's a goldendoodle, which is a golden retriever and poodle mix. Her name is Snuggles and she's hypoallergenic, which means she doesn't make Kelli's father sneeze as much as a regular dog would.

I hope it's not weird that I'm about to write what I'm about to write, but I also noticed that Kelli was wearing a bra. It would have been impossible *not* to notice, because her shirt was thin and her shoulder straps were peeking out.

Most girls in our class do NOT wear bras!

I doubt I'll ever *need* a bra, to tell you the truth. (Hey, the initials of "to tell you the truth" are T-T-Y-T-T!) But who knows? Pip and Kelli are growing up—so maybe I am too and just can't tell?

Anyway, the lady in the uniform, Mrs. Atkins, kept asking what kind of pizza we all wanted and offering different toppings, from *peppers* to *pepper*oni. I asked for a plain slice because my stomach was full of butterflies, and I wasn't sure if pizza and butterflies mix.

Well, I was in the middle of a bite when Chuck walked in. He wasn't dressed up (maybe boys dress up only for Halloween?), but he did look extra handsome.

Kelli bounded over and handed him a card. "Open it!" she said, all excited. I hoped no one was watching me watch them, but I leaned forward so I could see the card. On it, a pair of honeybees were saying, "BEE MINE!"

Chuck had a card for her too! It had a picture of a bright-green dinosaur and the words, "You're DINOmite." Even though it was misspelled, when I read that, all the butterflies in my stomach flapped their wings one last time and…died. Every single one.

Is this what jealousy feels like? If so, it is terrible!

I didn't want to be looking at them looking at each other, but I couldn't turn away. I wished he'd handed *me* the DINOmite card. But he hadn't, so it was like tiny sticks of dynamite were exploding in my head. It's just so hard to believe that they are each other's valentine.

I was standing there trying not to feel sorry for myself when Kelli flicked the lights on and off and announced it was time to play limbo. "I did it every day on vacation in Trinidad," she added. (That's an island. I looked it up.) We followed her to her family's giant "rec room" where she had set up two vertical poles with a three-foot pole between them. She said we would all take turns trying to dance under the horizontal pole without knocking into it or falling down.

A few kids looked confused, so she said, "I'll go first. Watch." Then she put on Caribbean music, leaned back so she was facing the ceiling, and with her knees forward, managed to step-step-step under the pole without knocking it over or landing on her butt.

Confession: I *wanted* Kelli to land on her butt!

"Who's next?" she asked.

Jamal said, "I'll go." But his shoulder bumped the pole, so he got eliminated.

Ethan said, "I'll try." But his chest bumped into the bar, so he got eliminated too.

"It isn't easy!" Kelli exclaimed with a lip-glossy smile. I thought that was obnoxious. Obviously, it *was* easy for her because of her gymnastics lessons and fancy vacation.

Grace, Olivia, Abigail, Aiden, Namira, Conner, Zara, Riley, Maham (whose name is a palindrome, M-A-H-A-M), and a bunch of others all went. Some made it under; some didn't.

"I'll try," Maybelle said. She leaned back, inched forward, and scooted under the pole.

I decided to get my turn over with, so I leaned back, stuck out my knees, and moved to the drumbeat. And I made it!

Chuck said, "I'll go," and made it look like it was a piece of cake, which we all knew it wasn't.

But here's what I have to tell you: when Chuck was practically horizontal to the floor, something fell out of his jacket pocket. A pack of bubblemint gum! When he stood up, he grabbed it really fast and jammed it back into his pocket. Then he looked at me, and I looked at him, and we kept looking at each other for a few really long seconds. (I know seconds all last the same amount, but some definitely feel longer than others.)

And I couldn't help wondering: Was that bubblemint gum for me? Part of me thought, *No, why would it be?* But another part of me was chock-full of hope.

"Who's next?" Kelli bubbled.

Emily J. bumped the pole with her tummy.

Emily S. bumped it with her chin.

Emily L. bumped it with her forehead.

Kelli kept saying, "How low can you go? How low can you go?" and kids kept getting eliminated. After each round, Kelli lowered the pole a smidge so it got even harder to slither under.

On my third turn, I lost my balance—splat!—so that was that. I was out. It made me mad that Kelli had invited us all to play a game she's so good at. Limbo is easy-peasy for her. She's been practicing. Her parents probably hired a limbo coach. (She really does have a homework helper who comes to her house every week, which I don't think is fair!)

Question: Did I lose my balance because I'm only so-so at limbo or because thinking about the mystery gum had made me dizzy?

Anyway, soon it was down to just Chuck and Kelli. Of course I was rooting for Chuck, but I have to say, they were both *naturals*, if that's the word. I guess Chuck and Kelli have limbo in common. But one difference is that every time she made it under, she seemed all proud of herself, and every time *he* did, he just looked relieved.

One good thing is that whenever it was his turn, I could look right at him without thinking twice about it, because everyone else was looking at him too. (I wish I didn't like looking at him as much as I do like looking at him.)

After two more rounds, Kelli whispered in his ear, he nodded, and they called it a tie. We all clapped, and Kelli's mom rushed over and took a million photos of the Limbo King and Queen. I wondered if she was going to post them or frame them—or both! Right when I was sick to death of clapping, Kelli's mom brought out pink mini cupcakes from Angel Cakes, the fanciest bakery in Misty Oaks. And Mrs. Atkins brought out chocolate-covered strawberries!

Soon parents started coming, and Kelli stepped outside to say good-bye to everyone.

I went to Kelli's bedroom to get my coat. Her room is pink and has a private bathroom with a lavender shower curtain dotted with bunnies. Part of me wanted to roll my eyes, but if I had my own private bathroom, I might not mind having a lavender shower curtain dotted with bunnies either.

I grabbed my coat and was about to scoot out the door when Chuck said, "Ava."

We hadn't said two words to each other all night.

"Yes," I said quietly.

"Remember at the bank, you said I could buy—?"

"I was kidding…" I interrupted, because I didn't want to say, "Of course I remember! I even wrote the conversation down in my diary!"

He reached into his pocket and handed me the pack of gum.

And I took it.

I took it!

And I know a pack of gum is *not* the same as a Valentine card with honeybees or dinosaurs or red roses or cutout letters. But bubblemint *is* sweet and so is Chuck.

I couldn't help smiling as I pictured him going to a store for gum and paying for it with his own money and knowing the whole time he was going to give it to me, me, me.

"Thank you," I said, and we looked at each other. I was feeling nervous but happy-nervous.

Just then, Kelli burst back in. Her blond hair was staticky and her cheeks were pink, and she saw us smiling. "Wasn't that super fun?" she asked.

I felt like she'd caught us breaking some rule, but she said, "Chuck, you're really great at limbo! I bet you're a great dancer too!"

"I've never really danced," he replied.

"I take classes every Thursday," she said, maybe hoping he'd sign up and they could learn cool new dance moves together.

He nodded, and I put the pack of gum into my pocket and touched it with my fingertips. It felt like a secret, and I made a decision: I might never even chew it. I might just *keep* it forever.

AVA, WITH A SECRET

Dear Diary,

When Pip came home, I asked about her date, and she said it went great. I said, "*Date* and *great* rhyme."

She ignored me and said, "But I'm starting to get really worried about the assembly."

"What do you mean?"

"Do you think Tanya and I should pick a different artist?"

"Why?"

"Well, when Maybelle saw our *Mona Lisa*, she laughed. Remember?"

"She didn't *mean* to be *mean*," I said, defending my best friend.

"I know, but maybe I should email Señor Sánchez and say we want to switch."

I thought about all the time Pip and Tanya had put into their project. "You already worked pretty hard on Botero."

"I know."

"And it's normal to be nervous, right?"

"I guess."

"It'll go great," I said because I was trying to be supportive.

"I hope so."
And I hoped I was giving her good advice.

AVA, ADVISING

DEAR DIARY,

I just put the bubblemint gum in the drawer of my bedside table and I felt really happy. But then I started wondering if Chuck bought me the gum at the same time as he bought Kelli the dino card. And if he did, which did he buy first?

Or let me put it this way: Why did he go to the store? Did he go to buy Kelli a card or to buy me the gum? Was one of us an *afterthought*?

AVA, AFTERTHOUGHT?

DEAR DIARY,

I've been thinking about the Aesop fable "The Fox and the Stork":

A fox invites a stork for dinner. The stork arrives hungry, and the fox sets out a yummy broth in a shallow dish. The fox laps it up, but all the stork can do is moisten the tip of his long bill. The fox says, "What's the matter? Did I make it too spicy?" The stork says no and invites the fox to come to his house. The following week, the fox sees that the stork has prepared a tasty fish soup, which he serves in a tall jar with a narrow neck. The stork eats it cheerfully, but all the fox can do is sniff it. So this time the fox is the one who goes home hungry.

The moral? "Beware of neighbors who play tricks."

I don't think Kelli was *tricking* us with the limbo party. But then again, I can't imagine inviting the whole grade over to play Boggle or do word scrambles or have a spelling bee. Just because you are good at something doesn't mean you should be a show-off about it!

Speaking of neighbors, the twins, Carmen and Lucia, who live next door and are in fourth grade, invited Pip and me over. We decided to dress in the same color since that's what *they* always do. (We picked green.) Pip is taking her Spanish homework with her so she can ask them a question. Funny that the twins can be homework helpers in Spanish even though they're years younger. Their parents are from Peru and always speak with them in *español*. I wonder if they'll think it's funny that we "copied" them by dressing in the same color.

AVA (AND AESOP)

Dear Diary,

When Carmen and Lucia answered their door, they were wearing green too, so we took selfies of all four of us in matching *verde* (that's green in *español*). Then the twins did something immature. They stuck tennis balls under their shirts so it would look like they had B-O-O-Bs. Lucia said she knows a secret code where A=B and B=C and C=D, and if you write out the whole alphabet that way, our mom's name, ANNA, spells something inappropriate.

"What?" I asked.

"BOOB!" Lucia answered and cracked up. I laughed too. I couldn't help it.

One fun thing about hanging out with the twins is that we can all act silly sometimes. I mean, fifth grade can be very serious.

Back home, in Pip's room, I picked up Otto, the stuffed orange fish that stays on her pillow, and pointed out that OTTO inside out is TOOT.

Pip said, "*Inside out?* Ava, that's nuts."

I said, "NUTS backward is STUN."

Pip said, "Stop!"

I said, "POTS."

Pip said, "I'm not in the mood!"

I said, "DOOM."

Pip said, "Leave!"

I wanted to say, "EVIL," but that's not how you spell "leave" backward, so I just stuck out my tongue and left. I'd wanted to ask Pip for some big-sister advice, but I could tell she was not in the MOOD.

BWB (THAT'S AVA IN CODE)

PS If you decode DIVDL, guess what you get?

Dear Diary,

Since there was no school today, I asked Dad if we could take a holiday from Meatless Mondays.

He said no. He says he likes having a weekly excuse to come up with a new vegetarian dish, and besides, Americans eat too much meat, and we should all eat more plants and nuts. I was going to say, "*That's* nuts," but I didn't.

Instead I helped Dad slice the cauliflower, onions, and Brussels sprouts, and toss them into a bowl with salt, pepper, olive oil, and a spice called cumin. Then we put the vegetables on a cookie sheet and roasted them in a very hot oven until they were practically burned up.

Maybe I was starving, but to tell you the truth (T-T-Y-T-T), dinner tasted way better than it looked. It was actually pretty good. If it were a P-O-P quiz, I'd give it an 85.

While Dad and I were cooking and Taco was sleeping in a block of sunshine, I told Dad that in FLASH, Ms. Sickle said that one out of *three* American kids is overweight or obese, and that this was "dangerous" because obesity is linked with serious health issues.

Dad said that it takes a lot of money and time to make salads and good-for-you dinners, "whereas fast food places are everywhere and you can buy junk food in every convenience store."

"You mean junk food is almost *too* convenient?"

"Exactly."

He also said even most juices have too much sugar in them, but supermarkets are not really in business to provide people with "healthful food"—they're in business to make money.

"I never thought of it that way," I admitted.

AVA, NAIVE?

PS Dad also told me a funny sentence. Ready?

"You can tune a piano but you can't tunafish." Hehe.

PPS It's weird that Brussels sprouts has a capital B. I mean, you don't write "Lima beans," and Lima is a city too. (There's a Lima in Peru and in Ohio.)

DEAR DIARY,

Last night I looked online for more tips for Tanya. There's a lot of dumb stuff about miracle pills that can help you drop twenty pounds in a week (which doesn't sound safe or possible). And sites that say that eating bacon can reverse diabetes (which can't be true).

But there are also good suggestions. Like: "When you go to the movies, order a small bag of popcorn, not a tub." And: "Don't weigh yourself every day." And: "Avoid late-night snacks."

All the experts say to eat less and exercise more and that vegetables are good for you (and not just on Monday).

Bea would say that common sense is good for you—and not just on Monday!

Anyway, I worked on the tips and wrote some rhymes, and when I went to bed, I was cold, so I kept my socks on. Taco jumped up and joined me. I should have left him well enough alone, but I tried to get him to go inside the covers, and he ran away. And after that, he wouldn't come back at all.

This made me think of a metaphor: feelings are like cats. You can't always control them.

Example: I never meant for my best guy friend to become my hush-hush crush, but that's what happened.

AVA, WITH CONFUSING FEELINGS

PS I want to ask Maybelle or Pip or even Dad or Mom about this, but I feel a little bad about liking someone else's boyfriend. PPS Then again, I don't feel thaaaat bad. Should I feel worse? Or should I feel bad about not feeling thaaaat bad??

2/16
11:50 A.M. IN THE LIBRARY

DEAR DIARY,

Last night after dinner, Pip practiced her Botero talk once for Mom and twice for her mirror. She's obviously anxious. The presentation is seventh period, so on the way to school, I let her practice it again for me.

Now I'm in the library. Two eighth graders, Rorie and Valeria, are at the next table. I know who they are because Valeria is in choir and Rorie is the one who is big and scary and friends with Loudmouth Lacey.

Both girls are staring at their cell phones, and Rorie just said, "Did you like the photo?"

Valeria said, "Not really."

Rorie said, "*Hello!* I don't care if you *like* it. I want you to *Like* it!"

Valeria mumbled, "Oh. Okay. I Liked it."

"What about this one?" Rorie said. "Should I post it?"

Valeria said, "Sure."

Rorie said, "You'd tell me if I looked fat, right?"

Valeria looked too afraid to tell Rorie anything, but she nodded.

Rorie said, "Okay. It's posted. Now Like it."

Valeria touched her screen.

Rorie said, "Last night when I posted the picture of all of us, everybody Liked it *except* you."

Val searched in her cell phone. "This picture?"

Rorie sneered. "Duh."

Valeria said, "Okay. I just Liked it."

"About time!" Rorie glanced over and saw *me*! She gave me a nasty glare and said, "What are you staring at?"

"Nothing," I mumbled. I could feel her eyes burning a hole in my head, so I went back to writing in you and decided not to even look up at all until they both left...

Which they...

finally...

finally...

did.

Confession: I'm glad I'm not on Facebook or Instagram or anything. Face-to-face life is hard enough! Plus, my neck would hurt if I looked down at my phone all day.

I "Like" that when I write in you, it's just for me.

AVA, EAVESDROPPER

DEAR DIARY,

Brace yourself.

Remember how I told Pip her presentation would go great?

It did *not* go great!

It went *terribly*!

The entire middle school filed into the auditorium, and I sat in the third row between Maybelle and Zara. I was right behind Kelli, who walked in front of a bunch of people so she could scoot in next to Chuck. I was tempted to say something about the silvery sequins on her headband, but I didn't. (I may *think* rude things, but I rarely say them out loud. And yes, I know I sometimes *write* mean things in you, but that's different, because I'm the only one who ever sees them.)

Anyway, the seventh-grade French students went first. Two by two, they talked about artists and showed their homemade posters and other paintings. We saw kids by Renoir, lilies by Monet, and a circus made of dots by Seurat.

Next, two boys talked about Manet and showed a painting called *Luncheon on the Grass*. Well, that made everyone laugh.

Why? Because it was of people on a picnic, and one of the women was totally naked. And that's the *naked* truth! (Get it?) I was shocked that the teachers let us see this, but maybe some art is supposed to be shocking?

I also noticed that MONET and MANET are spelled the same except for one little vowel.

After the French teacher said, "*Merci*," the Spanish students took their turn.

Isabel and Nadifa showed a poster of melting clocks based on a Salvador Dalí painting. Bea and another girl showed a poster of a deer with a woman's face based on a Frida Kahlo painting. Two boys showed a poster of Aesop (looking old and tired) based on a painting by Velázquez.

Finally it was Pip and Tanya's turn. Pip talked too quietly into the microphone, but last fall, she would not have been able to talk in public at all, so I was proud of her. She was talking about Botero's life and saying he was born in Colombia and lived in lots of countries and got married three times.

Tanya went next, and her job was to talk about Botero's *art*. And everything was going fine until they showed their poster and some of Botero's famous paintings.

Maybe by then, everyone had been sitting for too long. Or maybe people thought it was okay to laugh because they'd laughed at Manet's picnic painting. Or maybe middle school kids just aren't good at being mature. (*I'm* not that good at being mature.)

Anyway, when the fifth, sixth, seventh, and eighth graders saw Pip and Tanya's chubby *Mona Lisa* and Botero's chubby *Mona*

Lisa, chubby king, chubby dancer, chubby bullfighter, chubby cat, and chubby dog, they burst out laughing. They didn't even try to hold it in.

What really got them was Botero's painting of a naked lady from behind. You could see her...*behind*! And it was *jiggly*!

It didn't help that Tanya was going on and on about Botero's "passion" for "volume and proportion and corpulence."

One boy yelled, "Just say it. He likes FAT PEOPLE!"

"And BIG FAT BUTTS!" another boy added.

A third boy made piggy sounds and said softly, "Like yours!"

I couldn't believe he said that!

A fourth shouted, "WIGGLE WIGGLE WIGGLE!" which is a line from an annoying but catchy song.

Everyone started *losing* it! Everyone except Pip and Tanya. They just stood there *frozen*.

Should Señor Sánchez have seen this coming? He *is* the teacher. But it's his first year. And what was he supposed to have said? "Tanya, given your size, perhaps you shouldn't present Botero"? He *couldn't* say that, could he? If he had, her mom might have called the school to complain—or sue! I guess he could have *removed* Botero's name from the hat, but would it be right if *nobody* at Misty Oaks School ever got to learn about Botero?

Should *I* have seen this coming? I now realize that Pip was right to have worried, and I was wrong to have encouraged her not to switch artists. I was trying to be nice, but would it have been better if I'd kept my big mouth shut?

While Pip and Tanya stood there mute, more and more kids

were laughing. Not Maybelle or Chuck. But it makes my blood boil to report that even though Kelli was in the second row, she was giggling. She was also elbowing Chuck, and I heard her whisper, "Tanya could *model* for Botero! Wiggle wiggle wiggle!" Chuck didn't answer, but here's the awful part: Tanya heard every word.

Her eyes got shiny, and I could tell Pip had no idea what to do. Fortunately, Señor Sánchez raced onto the stage and nudged Pip and Tanya to the right. Then he turned to us and said, "*¡Basta!* Enough! Presenters, *muchas gracias*. Students, please exit in a quiet orderly fashion and report to your eighth-period class. Now! Now!!" His eyes flashed with rage.

Tanya was trying to hold back tears. And she was doing pretty well. But then all of a sudden, she wasn't. She was crying—just *crying*. It was like she was having a mini breakdown.

I was glad they were off to the side, but to be honest, it wasn't the quietest mini breakdown anyone had ever had, and I felt terrible for her, because I think a lot of other kids heard her too.

Pip was talking to Tanya—probably trying to convince her that people were laughing at the *paintings*, not at *them*.

But Tanya wasn't buying it, I could tell.

She was hurt.

No. Worse.

She was *devastated*.

AVA, ANGRY AND ANGUISHED

DEAR DIARY,

At dinner, Mom asked Pip how the presentation went.

Pip stared right at me and said, "Okay."

I got the message and stayed M-U-M.

"Did people like your poster?" Dad asked.

Pip said the posters would be on display outside the language classes.

"How was *your* day, Mom?" I asked, because I knew that if I asked them a question, it would take the spotlight off us. Well, Mom started talking about a Dachshund that had "tangled" with a porcupine and ended up with quills in its snout. She also told us about a Manx cat (Manx cats have no tails) that had bitten a toad and was foaming at the mouth because the toad was a little poisonous, but not in a lasting way.

Later when Pip and I were brushing our teeth (and foaming at the mouth, but not in a lasting way), I asked, "Why didn't you tell Mom and Dad?"

Pip said, "I just didn't."

"I'm sorry I told you everything would be fine."

She spat into the sink and shrugged. "I should have talked to Señor Sánchez."

"Tanya was so upset," I said.

"Can you blame her? She didn't deserve that! I'm about to text her to make sure she's okay."

I nodded. "You know the saying, 'Sticks and stones can break my bones, but words will never hurt me'?" I asked. "That's the dumbest thing ever."

"True," Pip said. "Some words are sharper than knives."

I did not ask if this was a simile or a metaphor.

I also did not ask: "Why did Kelli say that Tanya could model for Botero? And how can Chuck like her??"

Instead, I decided to be positive (B+) and try to B helpful. I'd felt humiliated because of tagalong toilet paper. Tanya must be feeling so much worse!

Pip might have been thinking the same thing, because she asked if Bea and I had finished the Tanya Tips.

"Not quite," I said. "You sure she still wants them?"

Pip nodded. "Yes. She told me she wants to lose weight but doesn't know how."

"Okay," I said and used Pip's cell to call Bea. We set up a time to meet. And I told Pip that our tips would be worth the wait.

AVA, ADAMANT (THAT'S LIKE "DETERMINED")

Dear Diary,

This morning, I asked Pip if Tanya had texted her back. She said no. I said, "Maybe her battery died, like Ben's?"

Pip shrugged. "Maybe. But Tanya is also not one of those people who checks her phone every five seconds."

Just now, Bea and I looked at what we have so far. Bea liked my poems and said she had called her aunt, the psychotherapist, for last-minute ideas.

We worked and worked and finally finished a list for me to copy over. I told Bea I might write them out on a piece of paper for Tanya and on a poster for my FLASH class.

In English, Mrs. Lemons always says we should revise our work before handing it in. "You check yourself in the mirror before you leave home, right? It's just as important to check your work." Well, tonight I will check, double-check, and triple-check our list.

I'll also try to come up with a catchy title.

AVA, POSTER GIRL

DEAR DIARY,

I copied the tips for Tanya, and Pip decorated the page with lark-spur, morning glories, and petunias. (She's already up to Q in *Z Is for Zinnia*.)

I also copied them onto a poster, which I'll give to Ms. Sickle tomorrow morning. I'm pretty happy with it all. I feel like while Kelli made Tanya feel worse, I'm trying to help her feel better.

Oh, on the poster, on top of the tips, I wrote FIT OR FAT in big bubble letters.

FIT and FAT are another pair of words that are spelled exactly the same except for one powerful little letter that changes every-thing! (Like JOY and JOB. And MONET and MANET. And BABBLE and BUBBLE. And TOP and TIP.)

After I finished, Pip took a photo of my poster with her cell phone and printed it out. I'm now going to tape it in my diary.

I hope Tanya likes our tips. I put them in an envelope, and on it, I wrote: *Your friend, Ava.*

YOUR FRIEND, AVA THE WISE

FIT OR FAT

Want to lose weight?
What's on your plate?
Also try to think
About what you drink.

Ava and Bea's Top Ten Tips

1. Drink H_2O—it's free and has zero calories.

2. Eat less—but don't obsess. (That's a rhyme!)

3. Exercise more than you did before. (Another rhyme!)

4. Slow down when you eat. It takes twenty minutes for your brain to figure out what your mouth has been up to.

5. Watch your S's. Cut back on Seconds, Sweets, Snacks, and Sugary Sodas.

6. Watch your O's. Cut back on FritOs, CheetOs, DoritOs, TostitOs, and OreOs.

7. Be colorful. Enjoy red, orange, yellow, green, and purple vegetables and fruits.

8. When you get tempted to overeat or binge on junk food, brush your teeth, chew sugarless gum, or nibble on fruit, veggies, or unbuttered popcorn.

9. Find a workout buddy or go on walk-and-talks. You can also do sports or walk a dog.

10. Congratulate yourself for taking care of yourself, one day at a time. Y-A-Y YOU!

IN THE LIBRARY

Dear Diary,

I ran into Tanya in the girls' room and told her I liked her presentation—but she looked like I'd hit her with a pillow. "I was about to put this in your locker," I said and handed her the envelope. I hoped Pip was right and that Tanya knew I was trying to be helpful.

"Thanks," she said and skimmed the list. It was awkward. I guess it's one thing to tell your quiet new friend that you wish you could lose weight and another to have her little sister show up with actual suggestions after you've been laughed at in front of the whole middle school. But Tanya *had* asked for tips. And to be honest, ever since Bea and I made the Pip Pointers, I'd kind of wanted to do another good D-E-E-D.

I'd also been thinking that if I ever do get to write kids' books someday (my new answer to "What do you want to do when you grow up?"), maybe I could write one called *Ava Wren Does It Again*. Or I could make a series called *Ava and Bea* about two girls who go around solving problems the way detectives solve mysteries…

Tanya studied the handwriting on the envelope and looked up. "Whoa, Ava. *You're* the one who gave me that valentine?"

"Sorry," I mumbled guiltily. I hadn't even thought about disguising my handwriting. I'd forgotten that you can recognize people by their handwriting just as you can by their voice or haircut or…posture. I hoped Tanya didn't feel tricked.

She frowned. "It's okay. At first, I guess I was hoping it was from a guy. But then I thought someone was making fun of me."

"No one would make fun of you!" I almost blurted, but, well, we both knew that wasn't true.

Some people really are *mean*. You know the saying, "He doesn't have a mean bone in his body"? Some people have mean *skeletons*. Some could give lessons in mean. Kelli has a few mean ribs in her rib cage. And Rorie, that scary eighth grader, probably has a whole mean spine!

I looked at Tanya in the mirror and what I *did* say was, "Tanya, don't let those dumdums get you down."

She gave me a soft smile and said, "My grandmother says, 'Don't let the *turkeys* get you down.'"

I mumbled, "Gobble, gobble," which I knew was immature the second it came out.

But Tanya laughed and said, "Gobble, gobble" back. Then three other girls came in, so we left.

After that, I went to find Ms. Sickle. I showed her my poster and asked if I could put it up in the hallway. She said, "Sure," and complimented my handwriting. I would have preferred if she'd complimented the words themselves, but I could tell she was busy.

I hope people like it as much as they liked "The Cat Who Wouldn't Purr."

Ava, Attempting to Aid and Assist

2/18
STUDY HALL

DEAR DIARY,

At lunch, Kelli was sitting next to Chuck, showing him photos of her goldendoodle, Snuggles. I wished I were sitting next to Chuck talking to him about my yellow tabby rescue cat, Taco. (I also kept sneaking peeks at the back of his head and then telling myself not to.)

After lunch, Tanya came by my locker. "I didn't know you were making a poster," she said. "I thought you made the tips just for me."

I didn't know what to say. It was true that Tanya had inspired us, but after Bea and I spent so much time on the tips, we (I?) thought it would be okay to share them with other people too. Especially since I want to be a writer and Bea wants to be an advice columnist.

"Does it matter?" I asked. I didn't want Tanya to be upset.

She looked down. "I guess not."

"No one knows you had anything to do with it," I said, in case that was her worry. "Ms. Sickle has been doing a unit on 'health and body image.'"

Tanya shrugged. "I just kind of liked the idea that you two made the list for me, special."

"We did," I said. "We mostly did."

She nodded. "It's okay. Never mind." She went to her next class, and I did too, but I have to say, the whole conversation made me feel a little upside down.

ΑVA (THAT'S AVA UPSIDE DOWN)

2/18
BEDTIME

Dear Diary,

I read an Aesop fable and told it to Pip:

A conceited ass was braying insulting things about a lion. At first, the lion was upset, and he started to growl and roar and bare his teeth. But then he looked more closely and realized the insults were coming from a silly ass, so he decided to just go his merry way and not pay any attention.

"What's the moral?" Pip asked.

"If the person insulting you is a dumdum, try not to care too much," I said, and told her that I gave the tips to Tanya.

"Yeah, but it's easier to ignore one dumb donkey—or dumdum," Pip said, "than to pretend you don't care about a whole assembly full of them, you know?"

"I know," I said and felt sad for Tanya. It seems like school is just easier for some kids (like Kelli and even me) than others (like Tanya and even Pip).

A.

AFTER SCHOOL WITH TACO BY MY SIDE

DEAR DIARY,

Today was the worst **worst WORST**.

I don't even want to tell *you* what happened! It was so awful that in English, I barely said a single syllable (even to Chuck), and I was shaky during the spelling test, which, by the way, included the word *nightmare*. Chuck kept looking at me like he could tell something was wrong, but I couldn't talk about it. Not in front of everyone!

After class, Mrs. Lemons asked if I was okay, so I waited until the very last person left and then I started to *cry*! Which I hardly ever do in school! It was embarrassing, even though Mrs. Lemons was nice and gave me a hug.

Here's what happened.

(Actually, I still don't want to write it down, because then it will feel real.)

Okay, I got to lunch late because I'd gone by our FLASH room to check on my poster. It wasn't there! Ms. Sickle wasn't either, so I decided I'd ask her about it later. By the time I got to the cafeteria, Maybelle's table was full. Chuck was with You-Know-Who. And even Pip was with friends. I figured I'd put my tray down at a corner table by myself, and someone nice would come join me.

That is *not* what happened.

That big scary eighth grader, Rorie, sat down. Then Valeria sat down. Then Loudmouth Lacey sat down. So did Rorie's seventh-grade friend Jayda, who has red hair. And so did Mackie, an eighth-grade girl whose dog recently ate a rubber ducky. (Dr. Gross had to operate.) For one stupid second, I thought, *W-O-W. All these older kids are sitting with me.* I even wondered if they liked my new poster.

Then I noticed that not one of them was smiling.

Maybe I'm better at reading faces than books, because suddenly it was crystal clear that these girls had it in for me. I was getting…ambushed.

Rorie spoke first. "One question, Ava," she said. "Who made you queen of the world?"

"Yeah," Lacey said. "You get your picture in the paper, and now you're like an *authority* on everything?" She crinkled her eyes like a snake.

"'Fit or Fat'? *Really?*" Jayda asked. "Who says it's either/or! There are plenty of overweight people who are fit. And plenty of skinny people who are wimps."

"How strong are *you*, anyway?" Lacey asked. She shoved my shoulder, and the others laughed. I knew I should stand up and run, but I felt stuck. Powerless. It was as if I'd wandered into a movie—a *horror* movie.

Rorie said, "You're lucky you're in fifth grade. Otherwise we'd be having this conversation *outside*."

Lacey cackled. "Little toothpick thinks she's the body police." She gave me a push to see if I'd fight back.

Rorie looked at Valeria, and Valeria said, "Yeah. We don't appreciate you telling people what they should or shouldn't eat. Or how they should or shouldn't look." Rorie nodded. "No one gets to tell us how to live our lives."

"It's a free country," Jayda added. "If I want to eat a pack of Oreos, it's none of your business! No one asked you!"

I wanted to shout, "That's not true!" because Tanya *had* asked me. But I also wanted to leave Tanya out of this. She had enough to worry about. I wished I could defend myself the way I'd defended Pip last year when Lacey made fun of her. But I couldn't. I was crumpling before their very eyes. If we were outside, would they be beating me up?

"You know how some girls eat two peas and a lettuce leaf and call it lunch?" Jayda said. "*That's* what's really bad! That and the girls who throw up on purpose." She studied my face. "And just so you know, I'm *fine* with how I look." She put one hand behind her head in a sassy way. "In fact, I'm so *fine*, I could be a plus-size model!" Mackie high-fived her.

Rorie said, "Oh, and if you're looking for that nasty poster you made with your buddy Bea, it's in the trash, okay? We don't need twigs like you going around telling everyone they should be a size zero. You got that?"

I might have nodded. Or my face might have gone up and down. But really, I don't think "I" had anything to do with it. It was like I was *watching* this scene, not living it.

Rorie gave Lacey a look, and Lacey added, "And for your information, some people gain weight more easily than others. So watch how you throw around the word 'fat,' okay?"

The girls were all staring at me, and I wished I'd never titled my poster "FIT OR FAT." To be honest, I mostly just liked how the words "fat" and "fit" *looked* together.

Stupid, stupid me!

"And some boys *like* girls with curves," Jayda said.

That cracked everyone up, but to me, it seemed really random, because what did boys have to do with *any* of this?

Mackie spoke up for the first time. She's the one who knows my mom because her dog ate the duck. "Ava," she said, "you've probably heard about sexism and racism. Well, there's such a thing as sizism too. So you need to think about that."

Sizism? Is that even a word? How could I be a sizist? I am not a sizist! I made that list because Tanya asked me to and because Ms. Sickles had said obesity is *dangerous*.

Rorie jumped in again. "Here's the thing: you may think it's bad to be fat, but we think it's worse to be a shallow little *zero!*"

Mackie looked at me and added more softly. "Ava, the point is that it's not good to judge people's insides by their *out*sides."

I wanted to say, "I wasn't! I don't!" but my nose was tingling, and I knew that if I said *anything*, I'd burst into tears.

"People come in all sizes," Mackie continued. "Some are big and some are small, and so what? It's not what you look like—it's who you are that counts."

She glanced at Rorie as if to say, "Enough already."

Rorie shrugged, then turned to me and said, "Okay, we're done. But we don't need you judging us. So why don't you get out of here and let us have our lunch in peace?"

"And while you're at it, grow up!" Lacey threw in.

I wanted to say that I was *trying* to grow up, but instead I ran out of the lunchroom even though I hadn't eaten a single bite. I didn't see Maybelle or Pip or Chuck, but I did see Kelli. She was staring at me. And I bet she knew exactly what had just happened.

AVA, ZERO

DEAR DIARY,

I phoned Maybelle, but she was on her way to Kelli's for a sleepover with Zara. That made me feel even worse!

I told Dad what a horrible mess I was in and how in my head, I'd gone from hero to zero without passing Go. He said he and Mom already knew about it, because after I'd told Mrs. Lemons, she'd told Principal Gupta, and she'd told Dad, and Dad had told Mom. Now there's going to be a special assembly for the whole middle school on bullying and health and I don't know what else.

There was supposed to be a P-E-P rally next Tuesday, but it got postponed because of me. Kids like rallies more than assemblies, and I wonder how many people will know it's my fault it got postponed.

Probably everyone.

I never want to go to school again.

I wonder if I can fake being sick until summer vacation.

AVA IN AGONY

5:30 P.M. IN THE LIVING ROOM

DEAR DIARY,

Dad asked if I wanted to go to the Great Wall or the Kahiki. I said I'd rather stay home with Taco, and could we order in tacos? Dad said sure and sat down next to me on the sofa.

"Thanks, though," I said, and Dad patted my knee as if I were seven. He also said he had a cat joke for me:

Question: What's the difference between a cat and a comma?

Answer: A cat has claws at the end of its paws, and a comma means a pause at the end of a clause.

I tried to smile, but I couldn't, partly because the joke wasn't very funny and partly because I'm feeling too mopey.

Kelli once said her family likes to dine out on Friday, and what if I ran into Maybelle and Zara and Kelli in a restaurant, having a great time without me? I couldn't take it.

AVA, AILING

PS I thought I was Ava the Wise, but I am…other*wise*.

2/19
BEDTIME

Dear Diary,

At dinner, while we ate takeout tacos, Pip said that *her* poster got ruined too—and so did Bea's! Someone gave *Mona Lisa* a beard and wrote "Wiggle Wiggle Wiggle" on her chest! And someone drew inappropriate private parts on Bea's deer! And boogies under the deer's nose! And someone gave Aesop sunglasses and a goatee!

I said the art poster vandals probably weren't the same girls who ripped down my FLASH poster because those girls would never have written "Wiggle Wiggle Wiggle" on *Mona Lisa*.

Pip said, "So true, Nancy Drew!" which she used to say back when she was reading an old series about a girl detective. (Now she's reading a series about a lady detective. It starts with *A Is for Alibi* and *B Is for Burglar*, and there's a new book for every letter.)

We talked about who might have written on the posters.

We did *not* talk about stupid Kelli's stupid sleepover.

Are Maybelle and Zara and Kelli hanging out in Kelli's pink room? Are they eating chocolate-covered strawberries? Are they talking about Chuck? Are they talking about *me*?

I wish *I* were having the sleepover.

And I wish Chuck weren't Kelli's boyfriend, because if he weren't taken, maybe I could call him and he could help me feel better. I keep thinking about Rorie, and I do get some of what she and those girls were saying. But did they have to gang up on me five to one???

A IS FOR ALONE

2/19
TWENTY MINUTES LATER

DEAR DIARY,

I wanted to talk, so I walked into Pip's room and said, "Life is not fair."

Pip said, "Number one, you should learn to knock. Number two, I'm on the phone with Ben. And number three, life is *fairly fair* for you and me. We have food and shelter, and you should have more *perspective.*"

I made a face and left. She didn't used to have *any* perspective, so who is she to criticize?

Writing things down usually helps, but tonight I also wanted to *talk.* I'm only human. And only eleven.

AVA, ARRRGGGH

PS I wish I'd never written those Tanya Tips. I'm having a hard time not giving myself a hard time!

MORNING, SQUEAKY CLEAN

DEAR DIARY,

I'm glad it's Saturday. I don't have it in me to even think about going back to school yet.

I don't even feel like writing in you.

I feel like soaking in a hot bath until it's not hot anymore, then draining out the water, turning the hot water back on, and taking an even longer bath.

But I already did that! I took the world's longest bath! By the time I got out, my fingers and toes were crinkly. (I'm lucky Pip didn't want to shower right after me, because when I use up all the hot water, she loses *all* perspective.)

The thing is, it's upsetting to have people upset with me. I wish I could wash away the bad feelings!

And it's hard to have "perspective," because I mostly see things through my own two eyes. Doesn't everyone?

Yesterday at school, it felt like all eyes were on me. Like I was at the eye of a storm.

A-V-A, E-Y-E?

2/21
LATE AFTERNOON

DEAR DIARY,

Dad made his famous Irish breakfast, and Pip told us she dreamed that *Z Is for Zinnia* won an award. I said I dreamed that some big kids were about to beat me up.

"Oh, honey," Mom said.

Later I went to Maybelle's, and we watched a Disney movie. That helped take my mind off my troubles—except for the part in *Beauty and the Beast* when the whole town just assumes that Beast is terrible when he isn't.

I decided to ask Maybelle about her sleepover with Kelli and Zara.

She said it was fun. At least she didn't say, "It was sooooo much fun!" Maybelle knows it hasn't been easy for me to watch her become friends with Zara, and now with Zara's friend Kelli— a.k.a. my…enemy? My *rival*?

"What did you guys do?" I asked.

"We watched a movie and went to the Great Wall," she said. (That made me extra glad that my family didn't go!) Maybelle looked up and added, "I will say this: Kelli's mom is a little—"

"A little what?"

Maybelle hesitated. "Well, let's just say she let us watch a movie that our parents and Zara's grandparents would *never* have let us watch. It was about a teenage girl who likes a boy who is a *bad* influence. And Kelli's mother, Candi—"

"Candy?"

"Candi with an *i!*"

"Go on."

"She watched part of it with us and acted…inappropriate."

"What do you mean? You have to tell me!"

"She said when she was our age, she wanted to be bigger, you know, up top. And she showed us this exercise she used to do with her friends. They'd kick back their arms and chant, 'We must, we must, we must build up the bust. The bigger, the better, the tighter the sweater, the boys will look at us!'"

"Omigod!"

"I know!"

"What did you and Zara do?"

"What could we do?"

"Didn't Kelli make her stop? Or tell her she was being, I don't know, sexist and sizist and…weird?"

"I don't think Kelli realized how weird it was. All she said was, 'Did it work?'"

"What did her mom say?"

"Of course not."

"Do *you* call her Candi?"

"Of course not!" Maybelle repeated.

I nodded and thought, *My mom may not be the huggiest mom in the world, but at least she's not embarrassing with a capital E.*

Back home, Mom was reading in bed and said, "Come in," so I did. I even got in next to her. She asked me what had caused "all the fuss" at school. So I told her that Tanya got laughed at in assembly, and I got *ostracized* (spelling word) in the cafeteria. She asked me to show her the Tanya Tips, so I did, explaining that I hadn't called anyone "fat," and Rorie had taken everything personally.

Mom nodded, and for a second, I wished she would give me a big hug and say all the right words like TV moms do. But Mom isn't like that. Her mom, Nana Ethel, isn't either.

Here's what Mom did say: "People get very sensitive about this subject. It's a minefield. Even Dr. Gross has to be super-careful when he tells clients that their cats or dogs need to lose weight." She looked at me. "He avoids saying 'fat' because it's such a loaded word."

"Like a loaded gun?"

"Well, not *that* dangerous." She met my eyes. "And not as dangerous as a real minefield either."

I pointed out that the word *diet* has the word *die* in it.

Mom chuckled. "Even for animals," she said, "losing weight is harder than you'd think. It's mostly up to the owner to buy special foods, provide exercise, and hold back on table scraps. No one wants to hear that their pet should go on a diet, but if an owner wants a pet to live a good, long life…"

Just then, Taco nudged the door open with his head, padded

toward us, and jumped onto the bed. Mom and I started petting him, and after a moment, Taco started purring.

I like how sweet Mom is with Taco. I sometimes forget that he's not only *my* first real pet, he's *Mom's* first real pet too!

"Taco's not a fat cat, right?" I whispered.

"Right," Mom replied.

"But he's not as scrawny as he was when we rescued him, right?"

"Right," she repeated.

"He's purr-fect," I said, and Mom agreed. I kissed Taco on his white zigzag.

"He's at a healthy weight for an adult indoor male," she added.

"You know the expression 'puppy love'? There should be a term 'kitty love.'"

Mom laughed. "You're right. There should."

AVA, RIGHT *NOT* WRONG

PS What I feel about Chuck may not be "true love," but it's more than "puppy love."

2/21
BEDTIME

DEAR DIARY,

I just read an Aesop fable that I wish I hadn't. Its moral is the opposite of the one for "The Lion and the Mouse."

That's the famous fable about the lion who gets really mad at the mouse who wakes him from a nap. The mouse begs the lion to spare him, and the lion says okay, and later, when hunters throw a net over the lion, the mouse sees him and starts gnawing away at the ropes and saves the lion's life. The moral? "No good deed is ever wasted."

Well, *this* fable, the one I just read, is called "The Frog and the Scorpion," and its moral is "No good deed goes unpunished." It starts out with a scorpion who begs a frog to ferry him to the other side of a stream:

"How do I know you won't sting me?" asks the frog.

"If I do, I will die too, because I can't swim," says the scorpion.

"How do I know you won't sting me when we get to the other side?" asks the frog.

"I would never do that!" says the scorpion.

The frog says, "Okay, fine," and the scorpion crawls onto the frog's

111

back, and they start across the water. In the middle, the scorpion stings the frog! His poison paralyzes the frog, and suddenly they are both about to drown.

"Why did you sting me?" the frog says. "Now we're both going to die!"

"It's who I am," the scorpion says. "I couldn't help it."

Worst. Fable. Ever.

I mean, I like how Aesop sometimes tells different stories to make different points. And I get that the world is complicated.

But still. "No good deed goes unpunished" is a terrible moral.

(Even if it might sometimes be a teeny-tiny, itty-bitty bit true.)

AVA, STUNG

2/22 (A PALINDROME DATE)
AFTER SCHOOL

DEAR DIARY,

Observation: when things are bad, you can tell who your friends are. Today a lot of people were *looking at* me, and a few were *looking out for* me.

Not Rorie. If looks could kill, I'd be dead as a doornail! She and her gang got detentions because they "harassed" me, and I bet she's blaming me for that—which is totally not fair. I also saw Lacey today, and she stared at me in a way that made me *want* to go hide in a bathroom stall!

Maybelle was extra sweet all day.

Zara was *too*.

And Bea was…*three*. In the hallway, she even said that those older girls had had no right to "dump on me," and there was "nothing wrong with our list." I was glad she didn't add, "Except your title," since *I* was the one who'd idiotically called it "FIT OR FAT."

Tanya actually left a note in my locker. It said, "Don't let the turkeys get you down. (Not easy, I know.) Gobble, gobble." She even sketched an excellent turkey with a droopy wattle and trusting eyes. An hour later, I left a note in her locker that said "Thanks!" and drew the only turkey I know how to draw, which is the kind you trace with your five fingers, the way we learned in first grade.

At lunch, Alla, a sixth grader whose name is a palindrome (A-L-L-A), told me that some of those same girls picked on her when she moved here from Russia. She also said that at her bus stop this morning, Tanya told her that her whole family is giving up soda.

"They are?" I asked.

Alla nodded and added that Tanya had asked her if she wanted to start taking walks after school.

"What did you say?"

"I said sure. So we're going to try to walk on Thursdays."

Okay, I am now about to tell you the best part. One other person was really nice to me today. Can you guess who?

Chuck! Yes, Chuck!

He and I got to English before anyone else, so we were alone for about one minute, maybe two. He said, "I heard what happened." I looked right at him, and my nose got tingly and my eyes got hot. "I wish I could help," he said.

"Maybe I'm just not cut out to be a writer," I said. I didn't expect to say that, but sometimes with Chuck, all I can be is honest. And after all, my writing *does* keep causing trouble, whether I write about a queen bee or rescue cat or weight loss. "I probably shouldn't be trusted with a pen."

"Ava, don't say that! You're a great writer! The S rule was funny. So was the O rule." He met my eyes.

"Wait! You saw the poster before they took it down?" Had Chuck read what I wrote about Seconds, Sweets, Snacks, and Sugary Soda? And Fritos, Cheetos, Doritos, Tostitos, and Oreos?

"I recognized your handwriting, so I read it on Friday morning."

"You didn't think it was bossy and offensive? Or that I was acting like the 'body police'?"

He shook his head. "I thought it was *sincere* and *earnest.*" He smiled because those were recent spelling words. "And brave," he added. "And…sweet."

He kept looking at me, and maybe this is all in my imagination, but it felt like he was thinking "…like you." And that he could tell I was thinking this.

It was as if we could read each other's minds.

"Chuck," I said, meeting his eyes, "you said you wished you could help, and I think you just did."

AVA, FEELING A BIT BETTER

2/22
BEDTIME

Dear Diary,

For Meatless Monday, Dad made kale quiche and a salad with fava beans, avocado, radishes, and quinoa. If I had to grade dinner, I'd give it a 75.

I don't get why quinoa is so popular, but maybe I don't understand popularity.

After dinner, I opened the drawer by my bed because I wanted to take a peek at my pack of gum. The one Chuck gave me. I thought it would make me feel warm. And calm. And happy.

Well, I opened the drawer and…the pack was opened! There were two crinkled wrappers and two missing pieces!

I barged into Pip's room without even knocking. "PIP!" I screamed. "What did you do?"

She was under the covers reading *I Is for Innocent.* "What?"

"That was *my gum!*" I said loudly.

She looked confused.

"You opened my pack of GUM!"

She stared at me. "Since when is that a federal crime?"

This might sound stupid, but since you are my diary and you

116

can't laugh or tell anyone, I will tell you what I did next: I started to cry. To *bawl*.

"Whoa, whoa, Ava, I can buy you a new pack," Pip offered.

"Chuck gave me *that pack*," I said, gulping. "You can't just replace it. It was special. It was"—I looked up at Ben's card on her bulletin board—"like a valentine."

"Chuck?" Pip asked, wide-eyed. "Chuck-Chuck?"

I nodded and felt like an idiot.

"You should have told me."

I shrugged, because what was I supposed to have told her? That I had a crush on my best guy friend since kindergarten, but he was going out with Headband Kelli? Or that Chuck gave me a pack of gum, and it felt like a present. And a secret. A secret present.

I hadn't told anyone. Not even Maybelle!

Some things are so private, I can only tell *you*.

What I *did* say was, "Pip, I have secrets too."

"I'm sorry, Ava, I didn't know," she said softly.

I nodded and finally said, "It's all right." I liked that lately Pip has been acting more like a big sister. "But *don't* take *any* more pieces!"

"Of course not!"

"Pinkie promise?"

"Pinkie promise," she said, and we hooked pinkies. And now I'm going to sleep because I'm tired as can be.

AVA, A TO ZZZZ

Dear Diary,

I asked Dad if I could stay home from school instead of going to the emergency assembly. He said no but offered to sit in the back if I wanted. I was about to say sure, but then I pictured Rorie and Lacey and Valeria and Jayda and Mackie making fun of me for having my "daddy" there to protect me. So I said, "It's okay." The words came out funny, because each one had to get around the lump in my throat. And because it was *not* okay.

Pip and I walked to school, and on the way, I asked if she knew who Kelli was. She said, "The pretty blond girl who's kind of full of herself?"

"Yes," I said. But then I thought: Aren't we all full of ourselves? Who else could we be full of?

AVA, TRYING TO HAVE PERSPECTIVE

PS Then again, I still don't get why Chuck even likes her. Does he truly like-like her? Why did she ever have to move to Misty Oaks anyway?

2/23
IN THE LIBRARY AFTER LUNCH
BUT BEFORE THE ASSEMBLY

Dear Diary,

It feels like everyone keeps looking at me. I think everyone heard that a group of older kids ganged up on a fifth grader and "defaced her property." But I think everyone also heard that the kid was an insensitive smarty-pants know-it-all who was so full of herself that she'd probably tell Santa to go on a diet. And I think everyone knows exactly who's who and thinks it's my fault the P-E-P rally got postponed. Which I guess it is.

Still, here's why it doesn't really feel fair:

1. I would *never* tell Santa to go on a diet.
2. I'm not insensitive. If anything, I'm *too* sensitive.
3. If Tanya hadn't *asked* for tips, I would never have come up with the list.

All I *mean* is, *well*, I'm not a *mean* person; I'm a *well-mean*ing person.

Since you're my diary, I will admit two things. Number one, I guess I'd been hoping that people would like our tips and Bea and I might even get a little recognition. (Is that a crime?) And number two, I did say something mean out loud today at lunch. I told Zara that I thought Kelli's rainbow headband was stupid-looking. I couldn't help it. It just popped out.

Instead of agreeing, Zara said, "But, Ava, why do you care so much? Maham wears colorful hijabs, and I bet you don't think twice about it." I looked at Maham, and it was true: today the hijab covering her head and neck is peacock blue, and other days she wears other colors, and I barely notice. (I used to, back when she first came to school.) And believe me, I realize that a head *scarf* has nothing to with a head*band*. But I could see Zara's point.

Then again, what did Zara expect me to say? *"I care about Kelli because I care about Chuck, and Chuck and Kelli care about each other."* Not a chance! And anyway, Zara may have halfway figured this all out.

The other reason why I've been obsessing extra is that I saw this on Kelli's notebook:

C
H
U
C
K E L L I

Maybe I'm a K-O-O-K, but I don't like that Chuck and Kelli have the letter K in common. He and I don't have any letters in common. Let alone limbo. Or sports.

AVA, MISUNDERSTOOD

2/23
3:30 P.M.

DEAR DIARY,

Usually when we sit down for an assembly, all you hear is everyone talking. Well, today, while we were finding our seats, Mr. Ramirez put on a catchy song called "Respect." When he turned it off, he told us that the singer was Aretha Franklin and asked us to spell out the word. So we did: "R.E.S.P.E.C.T."

"I can't hear you," he said, which was funny because as a librarian, he's usually shushing us.

"R.E.S.P.E.C.T.," we repeated.

"And what's that spell?"

"Respect!" we shouted.

"I can't hear you!" he said.

"RESPECT!" we shouted even more loudly.

"I still can't hear you!" he said, cupping his ear.

"**RESPECT!**" we yelled at the top of our lungs.

"That's right. And from now on, I want you to be more respectful of your classmates, yourselves, and other people's work. Is that clear?"

"Yes."

"Is it?"

"YES!"

No one snickered, and by now Mr. Ramirez sounded so serious, it made me wonder if *he* had ever been disrespected.

Next Principal Gupta stepped up and introduced the two speakers.

The first was a therapist in a suit and bow tie. He talked about *b*ullying and *b*ystanders and *b*oundaries, *b*ut he was *b*oring. Also, one of his pants' legs was twisted into his sock, which was distracting.

The second was a young nurse *practi*tioner whose advice was more *practi*cal and who had lots of twisty braids wrapped around her head.

"Your parents used to take care of you," she began. "Now you're learning to take care of yourselves." She said that chips and cookies have "empty" or "useless" calories, and we should eat real food and read labels and buy products with ingredients our "grandparents would recognize." She said little treats are fine, but if you get in the habit of "double desserts" and "emotional eating," you'll "jeopardize" your "long-term health" because obesity is linked to diabetes and heart and liver troubles.

"I'm not blaming or shaming," she said, "just sharing vital info. When it comes to weight, there's no magic pill, no one-size-fits-all advice." She said that kids have different body types and grow at different rates, and that some have "an easier relationship" with food than others, but we should all cut back on meat and sugar. She also said what Dad had said: that it doesn't help that food that is good for you costs more than food that is bad for you.

Soon it was time for questions, but I kept my head down, because the last thing I wanted was for more people to look at me.

A girl asked about anorexia, and the nurse practitioner said it is a serious disease, because if you don't eat enough, you can literally starve to death. She said bulimia is "life-threatening" too, because if you barf up your food, it can mess up your whole system, "even the back of your teeth." (She didn't say "barf"; she said "purge.") A sixth grader asked about skipping lunch, and she said, "It's better to have a glass of milk and a piece of whole wheat bread than nothing at all.

"Listen," she said, looking out at us. "I get that this can be tricky. Adults can say, 'Don't smoke' and 'Don't do drugs,' but no one can say, 'Don't eat.' You *need* to eat! So you have to learn to be *sensible* about it. If you need help, get help."

The therapist with the hitched-up pant leg took back the mike again. "I want to add that there's *not* a 'fine line' between *under-weight* or *overweight*. The majority of kids are in the middle." He looked out at us and nodded as if proving his own point. "And the goal is *not* to be thin—it's to be healthy and active and self-accepting."

I thought that was the end, but he said, "By the way, your principal told me you've been studying Botero." I could feel myself tensing up, and the whole room got a little extra quiet. Why was he reminding us of last week's disaster—not that anyone had forgotten? "Well, you might find it interesting that centuries ago," he continued, "if someone was curvy, that was prestigious. It was a sign of wealth! It meant that person wasn't going hungry. The painting *The Three Graces* by Rubens shows three very full-figured women."

For a second, I wondered if he was going to whip out a naked ladies art poster. But he didn't, and soon Principal Gupta hopped up and thanked both speakers. We all clapped, and as we filed out, Mr. Ramirez put the "Respect" song back on.

I bet I'll be spelling that word in my head for a long time.

A.V.A.W.R.E.N.

PS After school, I saw Lacey by the buses. She did not look at me *respect*fully. She gave me what Uncle Patrick calls "the hairy eyeball." So I tried to ignore her. Like the lion in the fable did to the a_ _.

2/23
BEDTIME

DEAR DIARY,

Maybelle called, and we talked about the assembly. She said, "Maybe I'm lucky, but I don't really get tempted to eat way too little or way too much."

"Same," I said. "Except on Halloween. Or when a tray of cookies is coming out of the oven."

"Kelli said her mom is a 'fitness nut,'" Maybelle said. "She spends *entire* mornings or afternoons at the gym—and she's not a professional athlete or anything."

I tried to picture Candi running on a treadmill for hours on end.

Maybelle continued. "My parents say, 'Everything in moderation, including moderation.'"

"I like that," I said. And then I *allllll*most told her I also like Chuck—but I didn't.

AVA THE MODERATE

Dear Diary,

Dad showed me a funny sentence on his computer: "English is weird. It can be understood through tough thorough thought, though." I asked him to print it out so I could show it to Mrs. Lemons.

We started talking about all the ways to pronounce *ough* and about silent letters in general. Like the *d* in *handsome*, or *b* in *dumb*, or *l* in *salmon*, or *t* in *castle*.

Or the *g* in *gnat* and *gnu* and *gnaw*.

Or the *k* in *knife* or *knickknacks* and *knock-knock* jokes.

I wanted to tell Dad a knock-knock joke, but I couldn't think of one because, well, I haven't heard any new ones in a while.

AVA WREN (WITH A SILENT W)

2/24
BEFORE DINNER

DEAR DIARY,

Dad needed eggs, so I went with him to the grocery store. I grabbed some cans of chicken soup, but then I read the label, and there was so much sodium (salt) and so many strange-sounding chemicals that the ingredients sounded like a practice list for a spelling bee.

I put the cans back and picked out a different brand.

We were about to leave when I saw Chuck in the produce aisle! He was with his mom, so at first, I kept my distance. But then his very tall mom started talking to the very short butcher, so I gave Chuck a wave, and he walked over.

I felt a little nervous and blurted, "I have a joke," even though he's usually the one with the jokes. "What word becomes shorter when you add two letters to it?"

"What do you mean?"

"What word becomes *shorter* when you add two letters to it?" I repeated.

After a few seconds, he said, "I give up."

"Short! Get it? SHORT + ER = SHORTER!"

He laughed, and we talked about yesterday's assembly.

Suddenly my heart started beating. "Chuck?" I said. "Speaking of R-E-S-P-E-C-T, when Kelli told you that Tanya could model for that Botero guy, that wasn't very nice. And Tanya was *right there*."

Chuck didn't say anything.

"Do you really like her?" I asked softly. "Like *like-like*?" I couldn't believe I was asking him this. It's one thing for me to ask this question over and over in my head, but another to ask him out loud. "You two have been going out for sixteen days."

Omigod!! Now he knew I'd been counting!! I wanted to stay quiet, but more words came flying out. I wondered if I was putting my cards on the table (instead of holding them close to my chest). "I know it's none of my business," I said, "but not minding my own business might be one of my weaknesses. And I'm still sort of surprised that you two are boyfriend-girlfriend."

Part of me wanted to go racing down the aisle and dive behind the display of organic pancake mix. But another part wanted to hear his answer.

"Me too," he mumbled.

"Wait. *You're* sort of surprised that you two are going out?"

He nodded.

"I don't get it."

"Me neither," he said. "It all happened so fast!"

"Wait. What?"

"Everything! One minute, I was on the bus, starving because I'd overslept. The next, Kelli offered me banana bread, so I took some. And suddenly we were in homeroom, and she was asking if I wanted to go out, and I don't know… I think I checked the circle because I didn't want to hurt her feelings."

He was looking at his sneakers, but I was looking at his face, his cheeks and nose and eyelashes. If I were older, I probably would have given him a hug or something.

"But what about *your* feelings?"

He gave a tiny nod. "She does call our house a lot. Like twice a day. My mom doesn't like it." He looked over at his mom. "I tell her it's about homework—but sometimes I just say, 'Mom, don't pick up,' because I don't always want to talk." He looked back at me and added, "Kelli *always* wants to talk. Especially about her dog."

"Snuggles," I offered.

"Snuggles," Chuck repeated. His eyes were soft and brown. "And she always wants us to sit together. Like every chance there is."

He was frowning, but I wanted to do a happy dance right there in front of the lemons and limes. If I knew how to juggle, I might have been tempted to juggle the lemons and limes and clementines, all while balancing on a watermelon.

"Maybe you could tell Kelli that your mom figured out that her calls weren't about homework, and she got mad and she's making you break up?" *Omigod*, I thought. *Did I really just say that?*

"I don't know," Chuck mumbled.

"All I mean is, you checked a circle. You didn't sign a contract in blood."

"True." He looked like he was considering this. "Ava, you know what you said about not minding your own business?"

"Yeah."

"I don't think that's a weakness."

"You don't?"

"Maybe sometimes it's the opposite. Maybe sometimes, it's a…strength."

I almost said that STRENGTH is a cool word because it has eight letters and only one is a vowel. Instead I told *that* part of my brain to SHUT UP. "Chuck," I said, "just remember that *your* feelings count too."

I hoped it wasn't dumb of me to be giving advice when I'm not a psychotherapist and my advice isn't always right.

Then again, what are "friends" for?

Just then, his very tall mom came over with her cart, so I said hello—and good-bye.

AVA, OUTSPOKEN?

BARELY AWAKE

DEAR DIARY,

Did that conversation really happen? Or was it a dream? I *think* it really happened, but I also feel like I dreamed it…

Oh. Wait. Now I remember. I dreamed that Chuck and I were at a bank! We were laughing and putting coins in a sorting machine, but it was more like a vending machine, and packs of *gum* and *gum*my bears (!) kept flying out.

Dreams are funny, right?

G-T-G. Got to go to school!

AVA, DREAMY

DEAR DIARY,

After FLASH, Ms. Sickle said, "That assembly stirred up an important conversation," and asked if I had another copy of my tips.

"Right here," I replied and pointed to the page in my diary.

"Great!" she said, reaching for my diary. "I can type it for you if you like."

"I'll copy it over!" I said, because I was *not* about to hand her my diary.

"Even better," she said and gave me poster board and a Sharpie. I said I'd do it in the library during study hall.

"And maybe just leave off the title this time?" she suggested.

Duh! I thought, but said, "Okay." I did not add that I'd probably never use the word *fat* again for the rest of my life. I'd probably never even say "bacon fat."

I'm now in the library making some changes to my list. I even decided to add a new tip: "Try to be positive and not let other people make you feel bad." Mr. Ramirez peeked over my shoulder, so I asked him if he thought I should add that.

"Sure." He smiled. "Ava, I wish I'd had this list when I was a kid."

"Really?" I asked.

He nodded. "My aunt called me 'Chunky.' A few kids at school called me 'Fatty' and 'Fatso.' It was bad. I was glad when I finally figured out that for me, doughnuts and McDonald's weren't worth it. And also when I figured out I should steer clear of idiots and start hanging out with the people who were interested in what I was interested in."

I noticed that Mr. Ramirez wasn't skinny, just regular. Or, as that bow tie guy put it, "in the middle."

"When's your wedding?" I asked, because we're all excited that he and his boyfriend are "tying the knot."

"End of the school year. June 19."

"Cool," I said. "I bet it will be fun."

He smiled. "We're going over lots of details right now. The menu, the band, the flowers, the rings."

I nodded, even though I'd never thought about the work behind a wedding.

"Mr. Ramirez, do you think I might be a little bit sizist?"

"Sizist?"

"Mackie said that's when you judge people by how much they weigh."

He considered this. "I suppose a lot of people are judgmental about one thing or another. But with obesity, it's almost not fair."

"What's not fair?"

"Well, many people have secret problems, like addiction or gambling, and you'd never know it just by looking at them.

Obesity is there for the whole world to see. But it doesn't help when someone wags a finger."

"Wags a finger?"

"Scolds, reprimands, criticizes." He put on a fake frown and wagged his finger up and down, which made us both laugh. "Anyway, Ava, I know you realize it isn't 'fat' versus 'skinny'—it's *healthy* versus *unhealthy*."

I like that Mr. Ramirez talks to me like we are two thinking people, not one smart grown-up and one dumb kid. But I might be dumber than he thinks.

I reread my list and was about to write "Weight Loss Tips" at the top. But what if a girl had an eating disorder and was starving herself? Telling her to drink zero-calorie water and to eat less would be horrible advice. I was beginning to see why there were so many books on this subject. And so many contradictory messages!

I made a few more changes and finally finished the new version and copied it over. On the top, I wrote "Take Care of Yourself." I rolled up the poster and shoved it in my backpack. It stuck out a little, but that didn't matter, because I was about to hand it to Ms. Sickle.

AVA, NOT A REAL *AUTHOR* OR *AUTHORITY* (BUT NOT A BAD PERSON EITHER)

PS I'm going to ask Pip to take a photo of it so I can print it out and tape it in here.

TAKE CARE OF YOURSELF

Want to feel great?
What's on your plate?
Also try to think
About what you drink.

1. Drink H_2O—it's free and is good for you.

2. Exercise more than you did before. (A rhyme!)

3. Be colorful. Enjoy red, orange, yellow, green, and purple vegetables and fruits.

4. Slow down when you eat. It takes twenty minutes for your brain to figure out what your mouth has been up to.

5. Watch your S's. Cut back on Seconds, Sweets, junky Snacks, and Sugary Sodas.

6. Watch your O's. Cut back on FritOs, CheetOs, DoritOs, TostitOs, and OreOs.

7. If you get tempted to overeat or binge on S's or O's, brush your teeth, chew sugarless gum, or nibble on fruit, veggies, or unbuttered popcorn.

8. Find a workout buddy or go on walk-and-talks. You can also do sports or walk a dog.

9. Try to be positive and not let other people make you feel bad.

10. Congratulate yourself for taking care of yourself, one day at a time. Y-A-Y YOU!

2/25
AFTER DINNER

DEAR DIARY,

At dinner, Dad said he had a new palindrome for us: "As I pee, sir, I see Pisa." (A-S-I-P-E-E-S-I-R-I-S-E-E-P-I-S-A). Pip laughed, and I pictured a tourist boy looking up at the Leaning Tower of Pisa.

Mom scowled as if she didn't think this was proper dinner conversation, but talking about sick or hurt pets might not be either, and she does that.

Just last week, she told us about a cat that had diarrhea, and how the owner had to bring in a "fecal sample." Pip said, "Frozen P-O-O-P?" and Dad said, "Let's change the subject, shall we?"

I think one of the nice things about when it's just our family is that it *is* okay to talk about absolutely everything. Like revised posters or frozen P-O-O-P or even forbidden crushes. (Not that I've talked to M-O-M or D-A-D about my *new* feelings for my *old* friend!)

ABSOLUTELY AVA

PS I wonder if Chuck is going to break up with Kelli. I wonder if it's bad that I spend a lot of time wondering this.

PPS Pip just came in and said, "Nothing is impossible," and showed me that if you add a space and an apostrophe, you can change "IMPOSSIBLE" to "I'M POSSIBLE." I said, "H-U-H" and then I said that some things *feel* impossible.

DEAR DIARY,

Last night, Taco jumped onto my bed for a long purring session. He usually acts tough and independent, but sometimes even he likes to cuddle and be comforted.

Question: Do tough *people* have soft sides too?

Pip has lots of sides, and I see all of them. Before bed, I asked her if she had any art books with Rubens paintings. She said no but googled *The Three Graces* and up popped an oil painting of three large naked ladies.

Pip read about the painting and said that Rubens painted it in 1639, and the women were supposed to be Zeus's daughters, and the three graces are charm, beauty, and creativity.

"H-U-H," I said and told Pip that I'm not going to use the word *fat* ever again.

"A nicer word is 'zaftig.'"

"Zaftig?"

"Zaftig," she repeated. "You can also say 'Rubenesque.' Think you can spell that?"

I thought about it, then got it right. Pip said "W-O-W."

AVA ELLE, WHO CAN SPELL QUITE WELL

DEAR DIARY,

In English, Chuck said he saw my poster. "It was as *earnest* and *sincere* as last time."

"And it's *not* judgmental," I said, because I liked my new title and because *judgmental* was about to be on our spelling test. Then I showed Chuck that the "preferred" spelling of *judgmental* has only one *e*, not two. "Same as *acknowledgments*. No *e* after the *dg*." I wrote both words out.

Guess what? We took our test, and he got both words right! So he got an 80!

We traded papers, and I put a big star around his grade and handed his back. He looked right into my eyes and said, "Thanks."

I didn't know whether the "Thanks" was for the grade or the star or the spelling lesson or just because. But I smiled and was glad that Kelli wasn't there, because I didn't even try to look away.

AVA, HONEST

PS Maybelle was absent today because she has a bug (weird expression) and was home sick. (Not "homesick"!)

2/27
Saturday afternoon

Dear Diary,

I put on my coat and snow boots and went to Maybelle's to give her the schoolwork she had missed, including a "brain teaser" from our math teacher Miss Hamshire (a.k.a. Miss Hamster). This is it:

"A bat and a ball together cost $1.10. The bat costs a dollar more than the ball. What is the price of the ball?"

"Easy!" I said. "Ten cents!"

"No," Maybelle said. "Five."

"No," I insisted, though I should have known better than to argue with Maybelle about math. But maybe she was dizzy from being sick? "It's ten!" I said.

"No," she replied patiently. "Let's say the ball is a nickel. If the bat costs a dollar more, then the bat costs $1.05. Right?"

"I guess…"

"Well, there you go. If you buy a five-cent ball, and also a bat that costs $1.05, you've spent your $1.10. So the ball costs five cents."

"Oh." I changed the subject because my head was spinning. "What'd you do yesterday?"

"Mostly slept and watched TV," Maybelle said. "But can I tell you something really personal?"

I hoped she wasn't going to say that she got her period. Or that she realized that she has a major crush on Chuck. Or that she and Zara and Kelli are going to start a club.

"Sure," I said.

"I found three little hairs under my arms."

I tried to hide my shock. "What are you going to do?"

"Shave, I guess? I mean, maybe someday? I think I'm going to ask my mom."

I nodded as if any minute now, I too expected to find private hairs in surprising places and would consult my mom.

Maybelle also said that last night, after she was feeling better, she convinced her parents to let her look at the stars because it was really clear out. (Maybelle is the only person I know who thinks about nighttime weather as much as daytime weather.)

"And?"

"It was beautiful! All the constellations! And the Milky Way! Do you know that the Earth travels through space at 67,000 miles per hour?"

"No."

"But it travels *silently*! There's no sound in space!"

"Why not?"

"There's no air, so the molecules can't vibrate."

I didn't know what she was talking about, and she could tell.

"Ava, isn't it weird? We're just dots in the universe! Our whole solar system is miniscule when you think about all the other stars and galaxies out there."

"Maybe," I said. "But I still get all worked up about stuff."

Maybelle smiled.

Anyway, I am now home, and I can't believe I'm writing in you, my diary, about the universe and my BFF's armpit hair. But I am.

Funny, it feels like I'm sitting completely still at my desk, but when you consider how fast the Earth travels and how fast everyone is growing up, maybe I'm not sitting *still* at all.

AVA, DOT

DEAR DIARY,

I raised both my arms in front of the mirror, and I definitely do not have any armpit hair.

But you know what? I think Pip *has* started to shave. I noticed a pink razor in the back of the bathroom drawer! How long has it been there? Days? Weeks? Months?

AVA, ANALYZING

Saturday night

Dear Diary,

Pip finished *Z Is for Zinnia* and showed it to me. My favorite new pages are Q is for Queen Anne's lace, S is for snapdragon, and U is for umbrella plant.

"You know what I'm looking forward to now?" Pip asked.

"Getting it published?"

"No. *Real* flowers. Spring."

"Spring?" I repeated.

"*Spring!* Crocuses and daffodils! Purples and yellows!"

I looked out at our lawn, and it was brown with dirty clumps of unmelted snow that were gray and shiny on top.

"Hey, how are things with Chuck?" Pip asked.

"Better." I didn't say anything else because I don't know what's going on between him and Kelli. Then I asked her about Ben.

"His mom might let me work at the bookstore," she said.

"For real? For money?"

"No, not for money. But she said she can give me advance reading copies of YA books and I can write reviews for their website."

"W-O-W," I said, because that sounded perfect for Pip. (Not

for me. I would *not* want to have to read young adult books or write bonus book reports.) I lowered my voice. "Have you and Ben..." I began, "...kissed on the lips?" It just popped out.

"Ava!" she said but did not kick me out of her room. "Not yet," she finally answered. "But he did kiss me on the cheek."

My eyes went wide.

"And that's our secret, okay?" she added.

"Okay," I said, glad we had sister secrets.

A B C = AVA IN BED WITH CAT

PS When a boy and a girl kiss for the first time, how can they be sure they won't bump noses or do it wrong?

2/28
BEDTIME

DEAR DIARY,

This is *not* a leap year, so today was the last day in February.

This morning, the twins next door, Carmen and Lucia, came over in pink jackets. Pip and I were in our pajamas, but we got dressed, and I told them about playing limbo two weeks ago. They thought that sounded fun, so we took turns holding up a broomstick while one person tried to scoot under it. I started talking about how my friend Chuck is great at limbo. (I think I just like saying—and writing—his name.)

Carmen said, "Is he your *boy*friend?" and I answered, "NO!" a little too loudly. Lucia dared me to invite him over, and I said "NO!" even louder.

Well, Tanya texted Pip and asked if she wanted to go for a walk, so next thing you know, all five of us were in the park playing Frisbee. The sun was shining and the snow had melted, and I'd forgotten how good it feels to run around and not be bundled up.

I thought of a baseball joke that Chuck had told me and told it to them:

"Once there was a boy who kept wondering why a baseball was growing larger and larger…and then it hit him!"

Everyone laughed.

Tanya ended up staying for dinner (a first) and helped us make roasted vegetables with shrimp. While we were cooking, Tanya told Dad that thanks to me, her whole family has been trying to eat better.

"Really?" Dad asked.

"Yes," Tanya said. "I asked my mom to stop buying Pepsi and Oreos, and she thought that was a good idea and would save us money too. My little brother is mad because he's not heavy, but my mom said it's better for all of us." Dad nodded. "She even put Ava's tips on our fridge."

"With a refrigerator magnet?" I asked, trying to picture it.

Tanya nodded. She turned back to Dad. "Mr. Wren, Ava's gotten the whole school talking!"

"About me?" I asked, suddenly paranoid.

"No! About soda and vegetables and 'paying attention' and stuff."

Taco brushed against my leg to remind me that it was his dinnertime and I should pay attention to him too.

AVA, ATTENTIVE

3/1
IN THE LIBRARY

DEAR DIARY,

You know how some people are hard-hearted? When it comes to Chuck, I might be *softhearted.*

I got to lunch early, and so did Chuck, and he put his tray down next to mine, which he never does. I looked around for Kelli but didn't see her.

"Hi," I said.

"Hi," he said, and our eyes locked a little. (Can eyes lock a little? I just mean that I tried to look away but couldn't.)

I told him that Pip and the twins and I had played limbo over the weekend, and it was fun, but nobody was as good at limbo as he was. (Was that flirting? I did *not* giggle or anything!)

Our eyes locked again. They just did. It felt like there was something more we wanted to say to each other.

But the world of school came rushing in when Maybelle and Zara and all three Emilys came and sat down. Jamal too. (Do he and Zara like each other??) It was like our old "lunch bunch," but with…boys. T-T-Y-T-T, it was a little awkward.

I remembered that Dad had printed out a riddle for me,

and I'd stuck it in my backpack. "You guys, I have a riddle! Are you ready?"

Everyone leaned in, and to be funny, the three Emilys said, "Ready." "Ready." "Ready."

"Okay," I said. "I am the beginning of the end, and the end of time, and I am essential to creation, and I surround every place."

They guessed "air" and "God" and "infinity" and "life" and "death" and even "love." "Wrong!" I said. "It's the letter *e*!"

I showed them the paper and pointed to all the *e*'s.

After a while, Chuck said, "I have a joke about a kayak."

Zara said, "K-A-Y-A-K is a palindrome!"

"I know," Chuck said and smiled at me. I smiled back, and our eyes locked again, and I totally had to *force* myself to look away. "Two people were in a kayak," he began. "It was freezing cold, so they built a little fire in the bottom of the boat. But the kayak started burning up, and the people sank and drowned."

"I don't get it," said Emily J.

"That's not funny," said Emily S.

"That's sad," said Emily L.

"Let me get to the punch line!" Chuck said and pronounced, "So it just goes to show: you can't have your *kayak* and *heat* it too."

Everyone laughed except Kelli, who suddenly appeared holding a chair and wormed her way between me and Chuck. "Can you tell it again?" she said.

Chuck frowned a tiny bit but repeated the joke. She still didn't get it and said she'd never heard the expression "You can't have your cake and eat it too." Well, Chuck explained it, and she finally laughed, and I wondered if maybe some rich people *can* because they can buy two cakes, and then, when they eat one, still have one?

Lunch was *not* as fun with Headband Kelli there, so I said I had to go to the library. I knew that being here alone—well, alone with you—would help me relax.

Funny. Writing and petting Taco help me relax. Reading and drawing help Pip relax. Reading and cooking help Dad. And maybe what helps Kelli is prancing around with headbands on her head and putting cucumber slices on her eyes and calling Chuck's house and sitting next to him even though I was there first.

AVA AT SCHOOL

DEAR DIARY,

I went to Dr. Gross's after school because Pip and Dad both had plans and I'm not allowed to "go home to an empty house." Soon I might be. Mom said that when she was eleven, she used to *get paid* to babysit for her neighbors.

I said that I like when I come home and, for instance, Dad is cooking, even when it's a Meatless Monday (like today). I also said I'm glad Taco is always home now too.

Anyway, I was doing my math in Dr. Gross's waiting room, and I was asking Penny at the desk about her three cats (one has just one eye) and her partner (whose name is Henny, which is pretty funny, since Penny rhymes with Henny). I was also noticing the containers of dog biscuits and cat treats and Dr. Gross's framed diploma from vet school. (He went to Cornell.) Well, guess who walked through on her way out the door? Mackie and BowWow!

I thought about pretending I didn't see them, but it's a small waiting room. I thought about pretending I didn't remember she was one of the girls who ganged up on me, but how could I forget? And then *she* said, "Hi."

I said hi back and even asked if BowWow had eaten any more rubber duckies.

"No," she said. "And it's a good thing! My dad said that operation cost a fortune!"

I didn't know what to say, because it's not like I'm the one who makes up the price for rubber duck removal surgery.

"He's been eating everything else in sight though," Mackie said. "Dr. Gross said he's too sedentary, and I should take him for a thirty-minute walk every day."

I know how to spell *sedentary* and that it means being a "couch potato" (or, in the case of a dog, maybe "floor potato"). But I was *not* about to comment on BowWow's physique.

No way.

No. Way.

No. Way. José.

While I sat there M-U-M, Mackie said, "You know what? It'll probably do me good to have to walk my overweight dog." Suddenly Penny went to the back to check on something which meant Mackie and I were alone. She looked right at me. "Ava," she said. "I feel bad about the other day."

I stayed quiet.

"I should have told Rorie to chill," she continued. "I swear, that girl has anger management issues. She knows she has to get in shape. She can barely walk up two flights of stairs! She had no business dragging the rest of *us* into it."

I couldn't disagree. (Double negative.) So I mumbled, "She always makes me nervous."

Mackie laughed. "She makes everyone nervous!"

BowWow started licking my fingers, which tickled, and was half nice, half gross.

"BowWow! Stop!" Mackie said.

"It's okay," I said, because it was.

"Rorie made it sound like you were going around saying that you have to be skinny to be happy," Mackie continued. "She said you'd crossed a line, and we needed to put you in your place. And yeah, you're pretty young to be dispensing advice, but I read your tips today and they weren't malicious. They were basically no big deal."

I was glad Mackie said that, but I also felt bad for my tips. Were they "basically no big deal"? I'd worked hard on them!

"Anyway, I probably should have thought about it a little more before I piled on."

"Thanks," I said quietly. "I probably should have thought about it a little more before I made that poster."

She sized me up and seemed to notice for the first time that I'm just a harmless fifth grader.

"You're a good kid," she said.

"I know," I said, even though I hadn't meant to agree out loud.

Mackie laughed and said, "Brave too." That was funny because people sometimes say that about me, but I never feel brave.

Mackie dug into her backpack for her cap, and out came a little bag of Wise potato chips. She put the cap on and said, "I may regret this the second I do it, but let's consider it a science experiment." She dropped the bag onto the floor. BowWow looked at her, confused.

I was confused too. I looked down the hallway and hoped Penny wasn't coming back right away.

"Five, four, three, two, one," Mackie said, then stomped on the bag with her boot.

The bag popped, BowWow barked, and Mackie laughed.

"It worked!" she said. "I thought that mostly just air would come out, but I wasn't totally sure. Of course if all the chips *had* gone flying, BowWow would have licked them up. Still, that would have been a lousy way for him to start his 'weight loss regime.'"

"An un*wise* way," I said. The word slipped out, and I was relieved when Mackie laughed.

She tossed the smashed bag into a garbage can. "Well, no backsies. The real test now will be if I can pass the 7-Eleven on the way home and *not* buy a new bag."

I almost said, "You can," but I kept my mouth shut.

AVA AFTER SCHOOL

3/1
7:30 P.M.

DEAR DIARY,

We just had a Meatless Monday dinner, and it was *really* good. I'd give it a 95. If vegetarian food were always that yummy, I would actually look forward to Mondays!

Dad and I made it together. It was eggplant parmesan, and my main job was to peel and slice the eggplants. The skin was beautiful, shiny, and sort of midnight purple. Dad said the French word for the color—*and* vegetable—is *aubergine* and asked me to try to spell it. I hesitated because foreign words can be hard, but I got it right. Dad high-fived me.

Then he started talking about how he used to cook with his father.

"Back then, not many fathers cooked," he said. "Let alone fathers and sons."

He told me his dad started the tradition of Irish breakfasts and Sunday sundaes. "He loved a good meal," he said.

Dad doesn't talk about his dad very often, and I kept peeling because I wanted him to keep talking. All I really knew about my grandfather is that he died at age sixty, before I was born. And that everybody loved him. And that his hair was red, like Pip's. And that he was good with words and liked to come up with limericks and funny toasts.

"My father would have loved you, Ava. You and Pip." Dad put down his knife and wiped his tomato-y hands on his apron. "He'd have taken you to plays and ball games and maybe even Ireland. I just wish he'd...taken better care of himself physically. His heart was in the right place, but it had to work too hard to sustain his body."

"What do you mean?" I asked quietly.

"Well, it's possible my dad would have died at sixty of a heart attack anyway. But maybe if he'd taken the time to exercise a little more back then, he could have had a little more time now. And since *I'm* not as young as I used to be, I want to do what I can to take care of myself and of you three." He smiled. "That's why *my* Sunday sundaes aren't as big as his were. And that's why when we have cake, we have slivers, not slices."

"You're still pretty young, Dad," I said. "Maybelle's dad has gray hair." Then I added, "I wish I could have met your father," because that was less shallow. And just as true.

"He was the original word nerd of the family, you know."

"I know," I said.

Dad showed me how to dip the slices of peeled eggplant into a bowl of beaten eggs, coat them with bread crumbs, and fry them, turning them each over once. Next we made layers: tomato sauce, eggplant, ricotta, and mozzarella, over and over again until we ran out.

"You're becoming more adventurous with food," Dad said.

I said, "Thanks." And then I added, "And thanks for taking care of us."

AVA, ADVENTUROUS AND APPRECIATIVE

RIGHT BEFORE BED

DEAR DIARY,

I just reread an Aesop fable called "The Bundle of Sticks." It goes like this:

An old man who was about to die summons his sons to give them parting advice. He orders his servants to bring in a bundle of sticks, and he says to his eldest son, "Break it." The son tries and tries with all his might, but he cannot break the bundle. The other sons also try and try, but they can't either. "Okay, now untie the bundle," says the father, "and each of you take one stick." They do, and the father says, "Break it." Each son breaks the stick, no problem. "You see," says their father. "Union gives strength."

I've been thinking about the moral, and sometimes it's good to *unite*, but sometimes it's better to *untie*.

For instance, Rorie is *trouble*. Her clique is "strong," but in a bad way. They're "strong" and *wrong*. And I get that it's hard to say no to someone like Rorie—I guess it was hard for Chuck to say no to Kelli. But Mackie ended up feeling bad that she went along with Rorie, and Chuck doesn't like getting stuck on the phone talking about Kelli's goldendoodle.

So maybe when you say yes to someone you *should* have said no to, you sometimes wish you'd just plain said no in the first place. Like, it might be better to be alone than with someone you don't like.

AVA, ASTUTE

PS Pip told me a joke. Why can't a bicycle stand alone? It's two tired. (Teehee.)

3/2
IN STUDY HALL

Dear Diary,

First thing this morning, Zara came up to my locker and said, "Did you hear about Chuck?"

"What about him?" I asked

"I think he and Kelli broke up."

"Why do you think that?"

"Because on the bus just now, Kelli walked right by him and sat next to Max. And she and Max started sharing a sticky bun and laughing."

"Did Chuck seem upset?"

"Not at all." Zara gave me a smile.

I couldn't help it. I smiled back.

AVA :)

3/3
3:33 P.M. (PALINDROME ALERT)

DEAR DIARY,

I sort of avoided Chuck today because I didn't want to say anything stupid. Of course, now I realize that avoiding him was stupid!

AVA, AWKWARD

IN BED FIRST THING IN THE MORNING

DEAR DIARY,

Today is March Fourth, which, if I were playing the homonym game, sounds like March Forth.

Right now, right this second, I think I am *marching forth* into my future and that I am slowly but surely going from being a kid to being a *teen*.

Little by *little*, I'm getting less *little*.

Question: Are things between Chuck and me going to keep changing? Should I tell him that I know things changed with Kelli?

I don't want to ruin our friendship, because I like our friendship. But I'm also (I admit it!) curious and excited to see what might happen next.

I think this means I'm growing up. But is anyone ever really all "grown-up"? Are all grown-ups *all grown-up*?

AVA IN BETWEEN, AGE ELEVEN YEARS, TWO MONTHS, AND THREE DAYS

ON THE LIVING ROOM SOFA WITH TACO

DEAR DIARY,

Pip said that she likes to make *to-do* lists, but then likes to check everything off and turn them into *ta-da* lists.

She also said that Ben heard a funny palindrome on YouTube by a comedian named Weird Al: oozy rat in a sanitary zoo. (O-O-Z-Y-R-A-T-I-N-A-S-A-N-I-T-A-R-Y-Z-O-O.)

Here's another surprising palindrome: Dr. Awkward. (D-R-A-W-K-W-A-R-D.)

AVA, AMUSED

PS Today Chuck had a doctor's appointment so he missed English. You know what? I missed him!

3/5
BEDTIME

DEAR DIARY,

We had our Friday spelling test, and I got another 100 and Chuck got another 80, and we both drew giant stars around each other's grades. He said my spelling brains must be rubbing off on him, which is a gross image, but I liked how his eyes smiled when he said it.

I didn't want to pass him a note and ask him out, but what if someone *else* asks him out? What if someone asks him out this weekend?

None of the Emilys like-like him, do they?

Confession: I can't imagine why *every girl* in our class—and in our grade—doesn't have a crush on him.

AVA, ANXIOUS

Dear Diary,

I don't know what got into Mom, but we were all four in the living room (all five if you count Taco), and out of the blue, Mom said that if Pip and I wanted to invite some girls to sleep over, that would be fine.

"Like a slumber party?" I said. The last time we'd planned a slumber party, it had *not* gone well.

"More like a sister sleepover," Mom said. "You could each invite a couple of girls."

Pip was so deep into her new detective novel, *J Is for Judgment*, that she did not even hear us talking. Mom and I both called her name, but Pip did not react. Taco did. He was looking down at us from on top of a bookshelf—which was funny. He keeps finding new places to sit and perch. And sometimes they are way up high—as if he wants to be sure to stay out of the way of any random dogs or coyotes.

Well, Dad winked at us and said, "Watch." Then he called Pip's cell phone. It rang, and she looked startled but picked up.

Dad said "Hello!" and Mom and I laughed. Pip didn't. In fact, she was about to get mad when I told her Mom's idea. Next thing you know, we were inviting Maybelle, Zara, Bea, and Tanya over.

Guess what? They're all coming—with sleeping bags! We're going to have a camp-out in our living room! I've never had a slumber party with older girls before.

AVA IN ANTICIPATION

PS Should I ask the girls about Chuck? Would that be a *terri*fic idea or a *terri*ble idea?

3/7
SUNDAY AFTERNOON

DEAR DIARY,

We did not slumber much at our slumber party.

We played Pictionary (Pip and Tanya were the best) and charades (Bea and Zara were the best) and we tried to hold a séance with a Ouija board (but it didn't work).

After Mom and Dad went to bed, we raided the refrigerator and ate grapes, Twizzlers, and M&Ms. Mom and Dad must have *expected* us to, because they were the ones who bought the snacks, but it was still fun to be sneaky.

At ten p.m., Bea made up a game called Secrets. First everyone had to write out a personal question on a strip of paper and put it in a bag. Then everyone had to pick out a random question, answer it, and choose someone else to answer it. Then that person picked the next question—and next person.

I'm about to tape all six questions in here. We didn't tell which question we wrote, but *I* wrote the first one, and I will write down my guesses about who wrote the others. (Note: I was going to write, "Have you ever kissed a boy?" but I didn't want Pip to kill me if she picked it.)

QUESTIONS

WHEN WAS THE LAST TIME YOU CRIED? (AVA)

WOULD YOU WANT TO BE FAMOUS? WHY OR WHY NOT AND FOR WHAT? (PIP)

DO YOU HAVE A CRUSH, AND IF SO, ON WHO? (MAYBELLE)

WHO IS YOUR FAVORITE (OR LEAST) FAVORITE RELATIVE, AND WHY? (BEA)

IF YOU COULD CHANGE ONE THING ABOUT YOUR BODY, WHAT WOULD IT BE? (ZARA)

WHAT DO YOU FEEL GUILTY ABOUT? (TANYA)

We started, and I picked my own question (the one about crying), so I read it aloud then said, "At school right in front of Mrs. Lemons." Everyone nodded sympathetically. Then I chose Zara. She said she cried when her mom said she had to live with her grandparents. We stayed quiet in case she wanted to say more, but she didn't.

Zara picked the crush question and admitted that she likes Jamal! (Observation: when you like—or dislike—someone, it's pretty hard to hide.) I thought Zara might choose me, but she chose Pip, and Pip said, "Ben used to be my crush, but now he's my boyfriend!"

Pip picked the body question and said, "I wouldn't mind being taller than my *little* sister." She stuck her tongue out at me in a nice-ish way, so I quoted Dr. Seuss to her: "A person's a person no matter how small." Pip gave Tanya a questioning look, and Tanya nodded, so Pip picked her. I guess Pip thought it wouldn't be toooo awkward, because it was just us girls and we already knew what Tanya might say.

What she said was, "My goal is to lose twenty-five pounds, and I'm proud of myself because I've already lost four." We said encouraging things, and Tanya added, "I'm big-boned, like my mom, so I'll never wear a small or a medium. But maybe someday I can shop where you all do, instead of in special sections."

Next Tanya picked the favorite relative question. If Pip or I had picked it, we might have said that our Nana Ethel is *not* "one of those Hallmark grandmothers" and explained that she gives pat-pats instead of hugs and rarely sends gifts or asks about Taco or anything. But then we might have felt disloyal. So I was glad Tanya got that question. Tanya said her favorite relative is her grandmother, "because she always makes me feel beautiful."

Then she pointed to Bea, who, of course, said her favorite relative was her aunt the psychotherapist.

Bea picked the famous question and said she wants to be an advice columnist. (I now realize that I would *not* want to—too much responsibility and too easy to mess up!) Bea chose Maybelle, who said she wouldn't mind being an astronaut or the president of the Hayden Planetarium but added, "I also wouldn't mind being a regular math teacher."

Maybelle picked the very last question ("What do you feel guilty about?"), and since the other girls had already answered two questions each, I knew that I would also have to answer it too. Maybelle said she still felt guilty about the terrible haircut she gave me last year. I said I'd gotten two real haircuts since then and not to worry.

When it was my final turn, I looked at Bea and said that I still felt bad about writing "Sting of the Queen Bee," that contest story that had hurt her feelings. She said, "It's water under the bridge," which is an expression.

Well, I'd had a moment to think about guilt, so I decided to give some bonus answers. I looked at Pip and said I felt bad about practically giving away Taco last month without asking her and also about telling her the presentation would go fine when what did I know? I looked at Bea and said, "And I shouldn't have written 'FIT OR FAT' on our tips." I looked at Zara and said I could have been nicer when we started becoming friends. I looked at Tanya and said I was sorry I hadn't told her that I'd planned to turn her private letter into a public poster. Then I looked at

Maybelle, my BFF, and since I *still* hadn't told her about Chuck, I decided this was an excellent time to announce right then and there, out loud, to everybody, that I was ready to make a big confession. So I said that.

Everyone got quiet, and my heart was racing, and my mouth went dry, and I wondered if this was dumb. After all, I hadn't even *gotten* the crush question! But I made myself be brave and take a risk and just plain say it. So I took a breath and declared, "I have a crush on Chuck."

Instead of gasping in astonishment, they all looked at each other and cracked up. For a second, I felt like an idiot.

Zara smiled and said, "I think we all kind of knew that."

Bea said that I wasn't the first person to have a crush on a friend and that I shouldn't feel bad about *anything*. "Let yourself off the hook," she added. "That's what my aunt would say."

Tanya said, "Ava, I just hope he likes you back. He should."

AVA, SLUMBER PARTY GIRL

3/7
AN HOUR LATER

DEAR DIARY,

This morning, after Bea and Tanya left, Maybelle and Zara and I made breakfast snacks of banana slices topped with dabs of peanut butter.

Maybelle said that next Sunday is Pi Day and she might ask her mom if she can have a party too.

"A slumber party?" I asked.

"A *boy-girl party*," Maybelle said.

Zara liked that idea but asked, "What's Pi Day?"

"March 14," Maybelle said. "My family always celebrates by making pies."

"I don't get it," Zara said.

"Pi is 3.14159…" Maybelle began and then *kept going* until Zara and I, even though we were impressed, said, "Stopppp!" (And then, "Jinx!!")

Maybelle said, "Pi is a number that never stops. Every year, people celebrate it on 3/14—which happens to be Albert Einstein's birthday."

She explained that it's a letter in the Greek alphabet and drew the symbol π on a piece of paper for us.

"It looks like the three poles you need for limbo," I said.

"It does!" Zara agreed.

Maybelle laughed. "The point is we can have a party and make pies."

"What kind of pies?" I asked.

"Cherry, apple, coconut, banana cream. Whatever kind you like!"

I asked Maybelle if she was going to invite Kelli, and she said yes, but that she'd invite Max too. I said, "Good, because if she flirts with Chuck, I will throw a pie in her face."

Zara said, "I dare you."

"Ava," Maybelle said, "Kelli is not one hundred percent bad. Don't forget that you didn't like Bea right away either."

Zara added, "Or even me."

My mouth flopped open, but I realized I couldn't deny this, because I had been mad when she and Maybelle went to the circus and started hanging out. So I just looked at Zara and mumbled, "Sorry."

"It's okay." Zara laughed. "It's…water under the bridge!"

I thought about how Kelli had told Chuck that Tanya could model for Botero, "Wiggle Wiggle Wiggle," and added, "Okay, maybe I won't throw a pie in her face, but Kelli and I will never ever become besties!"

AVA, AT TIMES APOLOGETIC AND AT TIMES NOT

3/8
BEDTIME

DEAR DIARY,

At lunch today, I did something I've never done before: I sat next to Chuck! Emily LaCasse saw us and said, "Can I join you guys?" We had to say yes, but fortunately, she put down her backpack then went to get in line. So Chuck and I had about three minutes, just us.

"How's it going?" I asked.

"Good," he answered.

"Is that a new shirt?" I asked.

"Yes," he said.

I knew I should say, "It looks good" or "I like it" or something, but I couldn't and instead just stared at my chicken rice soup.

He took a peek at Kelli, who was wearing a short fuzzy white dress and sitting with Max three tables over. I peeked too. Max had two straws sticking out of his nose and looked like a moronic walrus, and Kelli was laughing hysterically. I wasn't sure if she was trying to make Chuck jealous or if she thought a boy with straws in his nose was the funniest thing on the planet.

"Is she still calling your house to talk about her goldendoodle?" I asked, then hoped that wasn't too rude or direct.

"No."

"Do you wish she were?"

"No."

"Am I asking too many questions?"

"No."

We both laughed, but not as hard as Kelli and Max. And I don't think it's because Kelli and Max were having much more fun at their table than we were at ours. I think it's because they are both just very loud. Maybe even *exuberant* (bonus spelling word). Come to think of it, maybe *they* make a good couple.

Suddenly Chuck leaned forward. "Ava, you were right," he said. "I should never have checked that circle. I didn't want to have a girlfriend. I mean, maybe when I'm in high school. Or *college*."

I nodded, waiting. This was not exactly the way I pictured this conversation going. Did he really *not* want a girlfriend until *college*?

He put down his fork. "Last Monday, she called three times in one day, so I finally told her that I didn't want to go out anymore. I tried to be polite, and maybe I should have done it in person? At least I didn't break up by text."

I half nodded.

"Anyway," he continued, "I did what you suggested: I blamed my mom and said she thinks I'm too young to go out."

I sat there, frozen. Whoa. Had I *suggested* that? Maybe I kind of had.

"Kelli and I don't have much in common," he added. "And we have totally different senses of humor."

I was *not* about to argue, *You're both good at sports! And limbo! And you both have a K in your name!*

The lunchroom was loud and so was my heartbeat. "But, Ava," Chuck continued, "if I *did* want to have a girlfriend"—he dropped his voice and I had to lean in—"I'd want it to be you."

At first I stayed silent. Then, when I knew I had to say something, I said, "Chuck, I don't want a boyfriend now either. But if I did…" Suddenly I stopped. I wasn't brave enough to finish that sentence! Not then and there anyway. So I started a new one. "Chuck," I said. "Maybe we can both *not* go out, but, like, *not* go out *together*. Like, we could be *not-going-out together*."

He nodded as though he understood what I meant even though it didn't really make sense. Then he said, "Maybe we can," and we both started laughing—but not hysterically or anything.

The Emilys came over, and Chuck made room by moving his chair closer to mine. Soon Maybelle, Jamal, Zara, Aiden, and Ryan sat down too. And just like that, we had an official boy-girl table, and it didn't even feel that weird.

"What's so funny?" Jamal asked, because Chuck and I must have been looking at each other as if we had a secret. (Which we sort of do.)

Without missing a beat, Chuck said, "I just told Ava the world's dumbest joke. Want to hear?"

"Sure," Zara answered for everybody.

Chuck gave me a smile and said, "There were two hats hanging on a hat rack in the hallway. One hat said to the other, 'You stay here—I'll go on a head.'"

Everyone half laughed half groaned (if you can half laugh half groan), and Bea walked by with Tanya and gave me a little thumbs-up, which, thank heavens, I don't think anyone else saw.

Now I'm home, and Taco is with me, and Mom and Dad and Pip are in their rooms, and I'm going to write down the words Chuck said to me, because I want to play them over in my mind. Like a song lyric.

Wait, I'm going to get my magic pen for this, the one Dad bought me at the Dublin Writers Museum.

Okay. Got it.

Here is what Chuck said:

"If I did want to have a girlfriend, I'd want it to be you."

We're both just eleven, and who knows about the future. But I'm glad that today we admitted that we like each other. Not that there's any big hurry to go public or get mushy or use the L word or think about *X*'s or *O*'s or *anything*. But still, I can't stop smiling.

XOX

AVA

PS After dinner, I checked to make sure my pack of gum was safe and sound. It was. It is. (Even though it will always be missing two pieces.)

3/9
BEDTIME

DEAR DIARY,

I can't believe I've almost filled up another whole diary! Neither can Mom or Dad. If diaries counted as books, I'd be *prolific* (spelling word alert).

Dad said he'd take me to Bates Books tomorrow to buy a new one. Since Dad is Irish, I teased, "You just want an excuse to see all the shamrocks."

He laughed. "Busted!"

Yesterday, Pip helped Ben and Mrs. Bates decorate the bookstore, and they hung shiny green clovers everywhere to get ready for St. Patrick's Day—which is March 17. Pip also helped two kids pick out books—*The Story of Ferdinand* and *A Fish Out of Water*. To thank her, Mrs. Bates gave her a magnet that says YAY! BOOKS!

When I grow up, if I do get to write books for kids, I might want to write a love story about two kids who are too young for real love.

Or maybe I can write about a girl who tries to do a good D-E-E-D, and at first it backfires, but then things work out, and she learns that what people say and how they say it both matter.

Speaking of, I hope Tanya keeps liking our tips and also that she can keep caring *about* herself enough to keep taking care *of* herself, if that makes sense.

Dad came to tuck me in, and we started talking about writing, and I said that one good thing about kids' novels is that they have happy endings.

"What do you mean?"

"Didn't you once tell me that plays sometimes end unhappily?"

"Did I?"

"Yes. You said that in Shakespeare plays, sometimes everyone ends up dead all over the stage. You said *Hamlet* ends up with a pile of bodies. And Romeo and Juliet don't get to go on a honeymoon or anything."

Dad laughed. "True. Until Disney came along, a lot of fairy tales had sad endings too. The way Hans Christian Andersen wrote it, the little mermaid turns into sea foam."

"Some Aesop fables have sad endings," I said. "The boy who cries wolf gets eaten up."

"Nom, nom, nom," Dad said as if he were a hungry wolf. He even *ululated*, which is a fancy word for howled.

"Stop!" I said, and he stopped. "You know something else about books?"

"What?" he asked.

"When an author writes a book, and someone buys it, the author still gets to *keep* the book. For artists, it's worse."

"What do you mean?"

"Like if Botero or Picasso or even Pip or Tanya sold a painting,"

I began, "they'd have to give up the original." Dad nodded. "Or take your plays. When the actors take the final bow, it's over. You can't play it again live in your office."

"Ah, but I can play it over in my mind. And when you write for the *stage* instead of the *page*," he said, making a rhyme, "you get to hear the audience laugh. Novelists don't usually get to hear readers' reactions."

"How's your new play coming?" I asked. I sometimes forget that not only do kids have ups and downs, but so do parents. (And elevators.)

"Pretty well," Dad said. "I have a new draft, and we're going to have a table read this month."

"A *first* draft?"

"More like a *tenth* draft!"

"What's this one called?"

"I haven't told you?" He looked surprised. "*First Love*."

"Is it autobiographical?"

"All writing is a mix of imagination, observation, and memory."

"H-U-H." Dad had once told me that success was a mix of *t*alent, *t*iming, and *t*enacity—I remember because it was an alliteration. "Has Mom read it?"

"Mom loves this play! And as you know, Mom can be a tough cookie."

"Can *I* read it?"

"Let me keep polishing it," he said. "Besides, you'll like it more when you're older." (Note: that's parent code for "You're too young.")

"Do the people in the play like each other the same amount?" I asked.

"Not right away," Dad replied.

"But it has a happy ending?"

Dad laughed. "It does."

"Are there any rivals?" I asked.

"Rivals?" Dad repeated, surprised. "I guess there are, actually. 'The course of true love never did run smooth.'" Dad smiled. "That's Shakespeare. Now lights out, okay?"

"Okay," I said, but then *negotiated* (spelling word) for five more minutes so I could write in you.

AVA...ALMOST...ASLEEP...

DEAR DIARY,

This is the last page of this diary. I'm about to put you on my bookshelf next to the other two diaries I finished.

Sorry I won't be able to tell you about the Pi Day party. It's in four days, and *everyone* is talking about it. Chuck and I have agreed to be pie-making partners, which, I confess, is about all I can think about.

Back in kindergarten, he and I were *assigned* to be apple-picking partners. This time, we *chose* each other. On purpose.

Funny. When I started this diary, I didn't even know I liked Chuck. Now we both know that we both like each other.

And the thing is: that feels like sort of enough.

For now, anyway.

Someday I might be ready for lip gloss and texting and phone calls and holding hands. But not yet.

At least not quite yet.

Oh wait. I just thought of something. This diary doesn't have a happy ending. What it has is (drum roll, please) a happy *beginning*...

AVA WREN, ON HER WAY

A Big Ol' Thank-You

It's true that writers write alone, but when I rewrite, I sure love company. And I appreciate when others help me, well, watch my language.

I am indebted to everyone who read my early pages and offered insight, suggestions, and sometimes even a joke or palindrome.

Here's to family: My mom, the late Marybeth Weston Bergman Lobdell. My husband, Rob Ackerman. My daughters, Lizzi and E-M-M-E. My brother, Eric, and his wife, Cynthia Weston. My cousins, Sarah Jeffrey and Matt Bird.

Here's to friends, teachers, interns: Sam Forman. Denver Butson and his daughter, the original Maybelle. Kathy Lathen and her daughter, H-A-N-N-A-H. Nick and Ginger Sander. Alan Frishman. Cathy Roos. Suzannah Weiss. Karolina Ksiasek. Katherine Dye. Claire Hogdgon. Jen Lu.

Thanks too to Tom Feyer and Sue Mermelstein, letters editors of *The New York Times*, who encouraged me to write a Sunday Dialogue about childhood obesity in 2014. And to Karen Bokram who invited me to be "Dear Carol" at *Girls' Life* back in 1994.

I'm beyond grateful to my fabulous agent, Susan Ginsburg,

who is always filled with the best kind of energy and to her wonderful assistant Stacy Testa, also of Writers House.

A giant bouquet to the Sourcebooks team—first and foremost my editor, Steve Geck. I am so glad he loves Misty Oaks as much as I do. A hearty shout-out to Heather Moore, Alex Yeadon, Sabrina Baskey, Nesli Anter, and Dominique Raccah. And an extra XOX to Victoria Jamieson who draws the charming book jackets, and to Elizabeth Boyer, who let me keeping revising even when it was time to say, "Pencils down!"

Finally, a nostalgic nod to my fifth-grade crush, Billy Hammer of Edgewood Elementary School, wherever he may be. And to Saul Ackerman, my Language Arts teacher, who made fifth grade so inspiring and memorable. A round of applause too, to all the booksellers who, like Mr. and Mrs. Bates, put books in the hands of kids.

Last but not least, a high five to *you*, because after all, what's a book without a reader?

About the Author

Carol Weston kept diaries as a girl. Her parents were word nerds in the best way. Her first book, *Girltalk: All the Stuff Your Sister Never Told You*, was published in a dozen languages and has been in print since 1985. Her next fourteen books include *The Diary of Melanie Martin* and three other Melanie Martin novels, as well as *Ava and Pip* and *Ava and Taco Cat*. Carol studied French and Spanish comparative literature at Yale, graduating summa cum laude. She has an MA in Spanish from Middlebury. Since 1994, she has been the "Dear Carol" advice columnist at *Girls' Life* magazine, and has made many YouTube videos for kids and parents. Carol and her husband, playwright Rob Ackerman, met as students in Madrid and live in Manhattan. They have two daughters and one cat. Carol's next novel is *The Speed of Life*. Find out more at CarolWeston.com.